THOMAS CRANE PUBLIC LIBRARY
QUINCY MASS
CITY APPROPRIATION

WORLD WAR II

Horrific Invasions

Marshall Cavendish
Benchmark
New York

Copyright © 2011 Marshall Cavendish Corporation

Published by Marshall Cavendish Benchmark
An imprint of Marshall Cavendish Corporation

All rights reserved.

No part of this publication may be reproduced, stored in a retrieval system or transmitted, in any form or by any means, electronic, mechanical, photocopying, recording, or otherwise, without the prior permission of the copyright owner. Request for permission should be addressed to the Publisher, Marshall Cavendish Corporation, 99 White Plains Road, Tarrytown, NY 10591. Tel: (914) 332-8888, fax: (914) 332-1888.

Website: www.marshallcavendish.us

This publication represents the opinions and views of the author based on the author's personal experience, knowledge, and research. The information in this book serves as a general guide only. The author and publisher have used their best efforts in preparing this book and disclaim liability rising directly and indirectly from the use and application of this book.

Other Marshall Cavendish Offices:
Marshall Cavendish International (Asia) Private Limited, 1 New Industrial Road, Singapore 536196 • Marshall Cavendish International (Thailand) Co Ltd. 253 Asoke, 12th Flr, Sukhumvit 21 Road, Klongtoey Nua, Wattana, Bangkok 10110, Thailand • Marshall Cavendish (Malaysia) Sdn Bhd, Times Subang, Lot 46, Subang Hi-Tech Industrial Park, Batu Tiga, 40000 Shah Alam, Selangor Darul Ehsan, Malaysia

Marshall Cavendish is a trademark of Times Publishing Limited

All websites were available and accurate when this book was sent to press.

Library of Congress Cataloging-in-Publication Data

Horrific invasions.
  p. cm. -- (World War II)
Includes bibliographical references and index.
Summary: "Covers the events of World War II from 1942 to 1943 including the Bataan "Death March," U.S. victory at Midway, the invasion of Burma, Stalingrad Airlift, and Operation Torch"--Provided by publisher.

ISBN 978-0-7614-4947-8
1. World War, 1939-1945--Campaigns--Juvenile literature.
D743.7.H67 2011
940.54'2--dc22

2010008624

Senior Editor: Deborah Grahame-Smith
Publisher: Michelle Bisson
Art Director: Anahid Hamparian
Series Designer: Bill Smith Group

PICTURE CREDITS
U.S. Army: Cover (YVONNE JOHNSON, APG NEWS), 96 (YVONNE JOHNSON, APG NEWS), 107 (Mary Markos [USAG Grafenwoehr]), 120 (USAMHI)
Associated Press: 20, 43, 73, 112
Department of Defense: 44
John F. Kennedy Presidentail Library and Museum: 59
Library of Congress: 16, 27 (U.S. Army Air Forces, Washington, D.C.), 108 (U.S. Army Signal Corps.), 116 (U.S. Army Signal Corps), 123 (Encylopedia Britannica)
National Archives and Records: 101
National Diet Library, Japan: 13
Naval History and Heritage Command: 7, 57
NAVY Amphibious Photo Archive: 35, 37
Robert Hunt Library: 4, 24, 38, 42, 50, 66, 80, 95
Science Museum of Maritime History Collections: 29
Shutterstock: 9 (Ivan Cholakov Gostock-dot-net), 11 (KumikoMurakamiCampos),

Additional imagery provided by U.S. Army, Joseph Gary Sheahan, 1944, Dreamstime.com, Shutterstock.com.

Contents

CHAPTER 1
Japan's Advance in the Pacific,
January to April, 1942 4

CHAPTER 2
The Tide Turns in the Pacific,
May to December, 1942 20

CHAPTER 3
Burma and China, 1942 to 1943 38

CHAPTER 4
War in the Pacific, 1943 50

CHAPTER 5
The Tide Turns in Eastern Europe,
1942 to 1943 66

CHAPTER 6
Occupation, Resistance,
and Collaboration 80

CHAPTER 7
North Africa, 1942 to 1943 96

CHAPTER 8
The Allied Plans for Victory,
1942 to 1943 112

Timeline 124

Bibliography 125

Further Information 126

Index 127

▶ Japanese troops on bicycles enter Saigon during the occupation of Indochina.

1 Japan's Advance in the Pacific, January to April 1942

KEY PEOPLE
- 🇺🇸 General Douglas MacArthur
- 🇯🇵 Admiral Isoroku Yamamoto
- 🇯🇵 General Masaharu Homma

KEY PLACES
- 🇵🇭 Bataan Peninsula
- Malaya
- 🇸🇬 Singapore
- 🇭🇰 Hong Kong
- 🇵🇭 Philippines
- Dutch East Indies
- 🇵🇭 Corregidor

The region most desired by the Japanese was Southeast Asia and the western Pacific. Both areas were controlled by other powers—Britain ruled Burma, Hong Kong, Malaya (now Malaysia), and parts of Borneo. The rest of the East Indies, including Sumatra and Java, were Dutch. The United States controlled Guam, Midway, and Wake, and governed the Philippines.

In September 1940 the Japanese occupied French Indochina (now Vietnam, Laos, and Cambodia). The French, recently defeated in Europe by Nazi Germany, could not fight back. The Japanese went on to develop a military strategy centered on rapid attacks. They used this across much of the central and southwest Pacific, including the surprise attack on the U.S. naval base at Pearl Harbor. Japanese leaders had great confidence in this strategy. One leader who raised doubts was Admiral Isoroku Yamamoto. He was responsible for turning strategic theory into operational fact. Yet Yamamoto suggested that initial successes would only delay, not prevent, Japan's defeat by the United States.

The Japanese plan of attack was put into operation in early December 1941. Less than sixty minutes after the December 7 (Eastern Pacific time) attack on Pearl Harbor, the Japanese began their attack on European possessions. They started with an air strike on Hong Kong, followed by an infantry attack across Hong Kong's border with China. The British defenders were caught off guard by the assault and within two days had retreated. They abandoned the city of Kowloon and withdrew to Hong Kong. The Japanese offered the British surrender terms on December 13, but these were rejected. Then the Japanese began an amphibious assault across the narrow straits that separated the mainland from Hong Kong. Two days later artillery, aircraft, and warships opened a bombardment. On the evening of December 18 the Japanese crossed the straits. Fanning out across the island, the Japanese smashed pockets of resistance. On December 25 the British were forced to surrender. The fall of one of Britain's most prestigious Asian colonies was an embarrassment. Apart from the loss of its naval facilities, all 12,000 British soldiers were killed or captured. The Japanese suffered just 3,000 casualties in little more than two weeks of fighting.

The fall of one of Britain's most prestigious Asian colonies was an embarrassment.

Prince of Wales and Repulse Lost

The British responded to war in the Pacific by sending the new battleship *Prince of Wales* and the battlecruiser *Repulse* from Singapore. The mission was to intercept Japanese ships bringing troops to the east coast of Siam (Thailand). The British naval squadron's commander, Admiral Tom Phillips, set out for the Gulf of Siam in the evening. But Japanese aircraft appeared overhead the following afternoon. Phillips knew that he could expect no protection from British land-based fighters, so he decided to return to Singapore by way of Kuantan on the Malayan east coast. In fact, the Japanese aircraft had not seen Phillips' squadron. But, thanks to submarine patrols, the Japanese were aware of its position. They were preparing a devastating attack.

At dawn on December 10, Japanese aircraft took off from Saigon (Ho Chi Minh City) in southern Indochina. At around 11:00 a.m. the aircraft opened their attack on the British warships. Only two of their bombs scored hits. Next came low-level torpedo bombers. Attacking from both port and starboard of the zigzagging warships, and avoiding a hail of antiaircraft fire, the torpedo bombers scored eleven lethal hits.

The *Repulse* sank at around 12:30 a.m. The *Prince of Wales* keeled over about an hour later. Accompanying destroyers rescued 2,081 of the 2,921 officers and sailors from the two vessels. The sinking of the warships was considered a disgrace. The Japanese lost just three aircraft, all torpedo bombers, and eighteen crewmen. This attack was the first successful one by land-based aircraft against warships at sea in wartime.

In this photo, taken from a Japanese aircraft, the *Repulse* (below) has just been hit by one bomb and near-missed by several more. The *Prince of Wales (above)* generates smoke after being hit earlier.

JAPAN'S ADVANCE IN THE PACIFIC, JANUARY TO APRIL 1942

Malaya Invaded

On December 8, two days before the loss of the *Prince of Wales* and *Repulse*, the Japanese Twenty-fifth Army led by Lieutenant General Tomoyuki Yamashita began to invade Malaya. Malaya held great value to resource-starved Japan. It produced around 50 percent of the world's rubber and 33 percent of its tin. It was believed that Singapore's supposedly great defenses could deter any invasion. Lieutenant General Arthur Percival, the British commander, had more than 100,000 men available. However, they were short of weapons and equipment. Also, they were also not used to the humid conditions. In contrast, although Yamashita had fewer men, they were well-equipped, had undergone jungle training, and some had combat experience.

> *Malaya held great value to resource-starved Japan. It produced around 50 percent of the world's rubber and 33 percent of its tin.*

After the air attacks on airfields in Malaya and Singapore, the Japanese landed at Singora and Patani in southern Siam and at Kota Bharu in northern Malaya. They made speedy progress down the peninsula's west and east coasts. The British mistakenly believed that the Japanese would stick to the few north–south roads and not move through Malaya's thick jungle. The Japanese moved skillfully through the jungle, and forced the British to withdraw or surrender. By early January 1942 the British defenses were crumbling. The Japanese captured Malaya's capital, Kuala Lumpur, on January 4.

The Allies then tried to bring some order to the defense of their Southeast Asian colonies. They established the joint ABDA (American-British-Dutch-Australian) Command under the British General Archibald Wavell on January 15. Wavell ordered Percival to abandon much of Malaya and retreat to Johor, the province at the southern tip of the Malayan Peninsula. The withdrawal was completed by mid-January. The Japanese, close behind, rapidly punched a hole through the Johor defensive line. Percival accepted that southern Malaya could no longer be held. He ordered his surviving forces back to Singapore on January 31.

British Humiliation at Singapore

The British were not particularly alarmed. Singapore was defended with heavy artillery. The single causeway connecting the mainland to Singapore had also been blown up on Percival's orders. New defenses were being built along the north shore, and the number of troops was being reinforced. Supplies were also believed to be plentiful.

The British completely misread Japan's strategy. Yamashita opened a devastating bombardment on the north shore. Then he began raids from aircraft based on Malayan airfields. The rain of bombs and shells continued for three days. On the night of February 8, the Japanese landed on the northwest part of the island. By the next day, the confused British defenders had abandoned much of western Singapore. The Japanese then stormed across the Strait of Johor to land troops near the destroyed causeway. The Japanese quickly repaired it to permit tanks to join the battle on the island. By February 11 virtually all of western Singapore was in Japanese hands. Percival saw that further resistance was futile. On February 15 he and his garrison surrendered to Yamashita. His swift victory won Yamashita the nickname "Tiger of Malaya."

The British completely misread Japan's strategy.

In around two months, the Japanese lost almost 10,000 men but had killed or captured some 140,000 British troops. The loss of Singapore remains Britain's greatest military defeat. It stunned both Churchill's government and the nation at large.

This type of Japanese propeller airplane assisted in the raids on the Malay airfields.

JAPAN'S ADVANCE IN THE PACIFIC, JANUARY TO APRIL 1942   9

The Dutch East Indies

Other air and naval forces were moving into the southwest Pacific. Their intention was to capture the islands of the oil-rich Dutch East Indies. The Japanese used bases in the Palau Islands, east of the Philippines, and Mindanao, in the southern Philippines. They did so to set up posts at Miri in Sarawak on December 16, 1941, and at Tarakan in eastern Borneo and Menado in northern Celebes (Sulawesi) on January 11, 1942. Troop convoys protected by warships and aircraft headed by way of the Macassar Strait between eastern Borneo and Celebes and through the Molucca Sea between Celebes and New Guinea. They wanted to take the Dutch islands of Sumatra, Java, and Bali, and the island of Portuguese Timor. A third point of advance into the Java Sea, through the South China Sea from bases in Indochina, was also developed.

Their intention was to capture the islands of the oil-rich Dutch East Indies. The Japanese used bases in the Palau Islands, east of the Philippines, and Mindanao, in the southern Philippines.

The Allies had few resources to oppose these thrusts. The bases used by the few available Dutch aircraft were under frequent attack; their ground forces were 85,000 troops scattered across the islands. Nevertheless, the remaining naval forces, mostly U.S. and Dutch warships, opposed the Japanese advance. On the night of January 23 a convoy of Japanese troops preparing to land at Balikpapan in southern Borneo was intercepted in the Macassar Strait. In sixty minutes four U.S. destroyers sank four troop transports and one escort. This was a minor victory, but it did not really slow the pace of the Japanese through the Macassar Strait and the Moluccan Sea. Balikpapan was occupied the following day, Kendari in eastern Celebes on the January 24, and the main Dutch naval base on Ambon on January 30.

Evidence came on February 4 that the two thrusts through the Molucca Sea and the Macassar Strait were close to linking up. At the Battle of Madoera Strait, northeast of Java, a combined U.S. and Dutch squadron was struck

JAPAN'S MILITARY STRATEGY

Japan had a well-planned military strategy to take control of the Pacific. But it had misunderstood what the political reaction, particularly of the United States, would be.

The Japanese Imperial Command had a three-stage plan to carve out an empire across Southeast Asia and the Pacific. The aim of stage one was to push rapidly outward from the Japanese mainland and the Japanese-controlled islands in the Pacific. The European powers and the United States had no more than 350,000 men at the outset to oppose 2.4 million Japanese army and 3 million reserves. They did not have a central command to control their operations. Meanwhile, the Japanese had a battle plan to integrate their land, air, and naval forces.

The second phase of the strategy was to fortify recently won territories as quickly as possible. Stage three centered on holding these new possessions. The Japanese thought that losses, actual or potential, could force the former colonial powers to accept the new status quo in Southeast Asia and the Pacific. The Japanese knew that the European colonial powers were weak and had few resources.

The United States was another matter. Although weak in ground and air forces in 1941, it did have a powerful Pacific Fleet, reserves of manpower, and the potential for a huge war machine. The Japanese, however, only addressed the problem of the Pacific Fleet. The surprise attack on Pearl Harbor would handle the problem. The fleet's destruction would lead to a U.S. declaration of war but also leave the United States without the naval resources to hit back. With few exceptions, most notably the commander of the Combined Fleet Admiral Isoroku Yamamoto, Japanese faith in victory was unshakable. The leadership simply assumed that the European colonial powers would seek peace as soon as they had been defeated in the Pacific. Then the isolated United States would conclude that fighting alone was too risky.

The Japanese failed because they were mistaken in their assumption that the European colonial powers would seek peace. They also had too much faith in an overwhelming victory at Pearl Harbor. The United States, it turned out, had just enough military resources to oppose them.

Imperial Japanese flag

by Japanese aircraft. Several ships, including the U.S. cruisers *Marblehead* and *Houston*, suffered significant damage. Australian and British warships joined the fight. But the new Allied force under the command of Dutch vice-admiral Karel Doorman was unable to block a Japanese invasion force on February 13. The port of Palembang in eastern Sumatra was occupied the next day.

Quickly moving eastward to prevent further Japanese advances toward Java and Bali, Doorman fought a night action in the Lombok Straits on February 19. Although both sides suffered damage and one Dutch warship was sunk, the pace of the Japanese advance barely slowed.

> *Allied intelligence had reported two invasion fleets heading for Java from southern Malaya and the Macassar Strait.*

The decisive naval engagement, the Battle of the Java Sea, came on February 27. Allied intelligence had reported two invasion fleets heading for Java from southern Malaya and the Macassar Strait. On board were 30,000 men of the Sixteenth Army, enough to overwhelm the 10,000-strong Dutch garrison on Java. Doorman was ordered to intercept the convoy leaving the Macassar Strait. He led five cruisers and nine destroyers. The Japanese escort squadron under Rear Admiral Takeo Takagi consisted of four cruisers and thirteen destroyers.

The Battle of the Java Sea lasted more than seven hours. The Allied warships were beaten off by Takagi's ships and by land-based aircraft. Two Dutch cruisers, including Doorman's flagship *De Ruyter*, were sunk, as well as one Dutch and two British destroyers.

All the other warships suffered damage. They withdrew to northern Java, where they refueled. Ordered to retreat southward, the *Houston* and the Australian cruiser *Perth* ran into a Japanese landing force and its escorts off Banten Bay on February 28–29 and were sunk. On March 1 the British cruiser Exeter and two destroyers were also sunk. The remaining warships, four U.S. destroyers, escaped to Australia. Left without vital naval protection, Java surrendered on March 9. The Japanese conquest of the Dutch East Indies was complete.

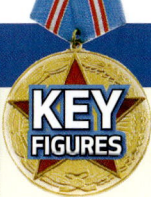

ISOROKU YAMAMOTO

Admiral Isoroku Yamamoto (1884 to 1943) was an outstanding naval strategist. He was the planner of the Pearl Harbor attack, and commander of the Imperial Japanese Combined Fleet from 1939 until 1943.

Yamamoto was a military visionary but also had a sharp political sense. He was an early advocate of a carrier-based naval air power. However, he also recognized that his country was not likely to win any conflict with the United States. He became unpopular for advising against war, but was nevertheless ordered to plan the Pearl Harbor raid. Yamamoto believed that the strike, even if successful, would not bring about total victory. It would only buy time for Japan while the United States gathered resources to counterattack.

Despite his growing pessimism after Pearl Harbor, Yamamoto continued to direct his country's naval and air strategies. He remained respected even after the Japanese defeat at Midway in June 1942.

Yamamoto fell victim to a U.S. intelligence coup in 1943. A code-breaking operation known as Magic discovered details of a proposed tour of the Solomon Islands in April of that year. As a result, Yamamoto's aircraft was shot down by U.S. fighter planes near Bougainville on April 18.

Admiral Isoroku Yamamoto

JAPAN'S ADVANCE IN THE PACIFIC, JANUARY TO APRIL 1942   13

U.S. Pacific Bases Fall

Other U.S. bases in the central Pacific came under attack shortly after Pearl Harbor. On December 8 the small garrison of Wake Island, 2,000 miles (3,200 km) from both Hawaii and the Philippines, was bombed by Japanese aircraft. An invasion fleet set sail from Kwajalein. Three days later these troops attempted to land, but 450 Marines and twelve marine aircraft under Major James Devereux fought back. Two Japanese destroyers were sunk and the invaders were forced to retreat. Wake was kept under aerial attack. The Japanese returned in greater strength on December 23. The Marines were overrun, and Devereux and his surviving troops were taken prisoner.

This map shows the Japanese attack on the Bataan Peninsula in January 1942.

Also on December 8 the Japanese launched air strikes from bases on nearby Saipan against Guam, one of the Mariana Islands. Although defended by 500 Marines and naval personnel, Guam lacked artillery. It was overrun in a few hours on December 10 after a 5,000-strong landing force arrived. Despite the loss of Wake and Guam, one U.S. base did survive. Midway, 1,100 miles (1,760 km) northwest of Pearl Harbor, would become a vital battleground in June 1942.

The Philippines

The defeats at Wake and Guam were followed by a even greater blow to the U. S. prestige—the loss of the Philippines. Japanese aircraft began to attack on December 8, but were easily beaten off. However, a second wave caught U.S. aircraft on the ground on Luzon, the main island. It destroyed some 50 percent of the aircraft and left most of the rest damaged. The Japanese invasion began with attacks on the north shore of Luzon on December 8 and at Legaspi on the southeast coast two days later. General Douglas MacArthur, commander of the U.S. forces in the Philippines, held the bulk of his units in central Luzon to meet the main threat. On December 22, at Lingayen Gulf on the west coast, 50,000 men commanded by General Masaharu Homma overwhelmed the Northern Luzon Force under Major General Jonathan Wainwright. He withdrew to the Bataan Peninsula. Manila itself faced severe air attacks. To save civilian lives, MacArthur declared Manila an open city, one that would not be defended. He withdrew to fortified Corregidor, off the southern tip of Bataan. He brought Philippine president Manuel Quezon and other officials with him.

The defeats at Wake and Guam were followed by a much greater blow to the U. S. prestige—the loss of the Philippines.

As MacArthur was establishing new headquarters on Corregidor, the U.S. and Filipino forces struggled to form a defensive line across the northern Bataan Peninsula. Key to this was to link Wainwright's command on Bataan and the Southern Luzon Force under Brigadier General George Parker. By the end of December, it appeared that the Japanese would crush

Parker, but a counterattack by the Northern Luzon Force opened a gap in the Japanese line. The remnants of the Southern Luzon Force managed to escape. The two corps established a 20-mile (32-km) line across the northern section of Bataan by January 7, 1942, but were too weak to hold it. On January 22 they fell back to a 12-mile (20-km) position 8 miles (13 km) to the south, only 15 miles (24 km) from the tip of the peninsula.

Homma gave his exhausted opponents no time to form a defensive line. On the night of January 23, his forces landed on the peninsula's west coast. These were repulsed by the local defenders, as was a further assault

DOUGLAS MACARTHUR

KEY FIGURES

General Douglas MacArthur

General Douglas MacArthur (1880–1964) dominated Allied military efforts in the southwest Pacific from the outbreak of the war through 1945. Controversial, overbearing, and sometimes arrogant, MacArthur was still an outstanding and dedicated general.

After the U.S. defeats in the Pacific during early 1942, the United States developed a two-pronged strategy to retake the lost territories. One thrust was through the central Pacific, while MacArthur led another drive directed from the southwest through the Solomon Islands toward the Philippines. MacArthur's strategy was based on leapfrogging attacks. In these, Allied air and naval forces gained superiority over their Japanese opponents, before ground units launched amphibious assaults against the smaller and weaker enemy garrisons. Main enemy bases, notably Rabaul on New Britain, were cut off, isolated, and left to "wither on the vine."

MacArthur's aim was the liberation of the Philippines, and the fulfillment of his famous promise "I shall return" when he left the islands. The islands were liberated in 1944. MacArthur was later made a five-star general, given command of all U.S. forces in the Pacific, and ran the Allied administration of Japan. His postwar career ended in controversy. He was effectively fired by President Harry S. Truman for wanting to use atomic weapons against China during the Korean War.

on January 26. An all-out push against the main defensive line on the following day was also beaten off. These costly assaults severely weakened Homma's command. The general was forced to ask for reinforcements on February 8.

Despite the resistance on Bataan, MacArthur realized that he could not win the battle. His command was almost totally isolated. Short of rations, equipment, and ammunition, it was only a matter of time before it was overwhelmed. However, time was something the Japanese did not have. Homma was expected to capture the Philippines in fifty days and then push on. Any delay would give the Allies time to prepare a defense of the Southwest Pacific and Australia. An extended defense of Bataan and Corregidor, however, could mean the loss of the U.S. and Filipino garrisons, including MacArthur. The U.S. government could not risk the capture of such an important military figure and ordered MacArthur to depart the Philippines. At first he refused but on February 23, President Franklin Roosevelt personally requested that MacArthur evacuate. After dark on March 12, the general, his staff, and senior local officials sailed for Mindanao, and took an aircraft to Australia. On March 16, as the battle on Bataan raged on, MacArthur made a radio broadcast promising the people of the Philippines: "I came through and I shall return."

MacArthur left the defense of Bataan to Wainwright, who established his command post on Corregidor. Wainwright, like Homma, recognized that his forces were reaching their limits. On April 1 Homma offered Wainwright surrender terms but was rebuffed. So the Japanese commander made an all-out effort to breach the Bataan defenses. Two days later, with air and artillery attacks the Japanese forces broke through. Eight days later, the garrison of about 12,000 U.S. troops and 64,000 Filipinos surrendered. Treated with contempt

> *The U.S. government could not risk the capture of such an important military figure and ordered MacArthur to depart the Philippines.*

> *...MacArthur made a radio broadcast promising the people of the Philippines: "I came through and I shall return."*

JAPAN'S ADVANCE IN THE PACIFIC, JANUARY TO APRIL 1942 17

by their conquerors, the U.S. and Filipino captives were forced to walk into captivity. This became known as the "Bataan Death March."

> ...Corregidor suffered heavy air raids and artillery bombardments. As the surface defenses were shattered, the garrison took cover in the caves...

Corregidor, known to its inhabitants as "The Rock," became the focus of the battle. Its garrison had 15,000 men, but with many ill or hurt, only around 1,300 were fit for duty. Food was in short supply. For the rest of April and into early May, Corregidor suffered heavy air raids and artillery bombardments. As the surface defenses were shattered, the garrison took cover in the caves and the complexes of shelters that lay beneath the island's coast. The coast continued to be attacked by Japanese forces

A series of victories left the Japanese in control of a large area of the Pacific by mid-1942.

18   HORRIFIC INVASIONS

THE BATAAN DEATH MARCH

KEY EVENTS

The surrender of U.S. and Filipino forces to the Japanese on Bataan in April 1942 was followed by a forced march to captivity. It left many prisoners of war either dead or too severely weakened to survive.

Some 76,000 troops surrendered to the Japanese on April 9 and began the long march under an intensely hot sun from Mariveles on the south coast to San Fernando to the north, a distance of 65 miles (104 km). Frequently denied food or water, the men stumbled northward, suffering beatings and other cruelties. Those who fell by the wayside were often bayoneted to death. By the time the ordeal had ended, 2,330 Americans and 7,000 to 10,000 Filipinos had died.

After the war, Bataan was considered a war crime. Its commander, General Masaharu Homma, was put on trial, found guilty, and executed in 1946. It was stated that he had not endorsed such brutality, and that the Japanese had expected only 30,000 prisoners and therefore had resources to care for that number. None could, or did, justify the treatment suffered by the captives at the hands of many of their guards.

until the night of May 5 when the Japanese landed troops on the northeast shore. These met fierce resistance on the beaches and many were killed, but Homma sent more men ashore. By dawn the next day the Japanese were fanning out across the island, cutting the defenders' telephone lines and seizing the water supply. Wainwright had no choice but to surrender.

> *The Japanese moved swiftly to occupy the rest of the Philippines.*

The Japanese moved swiftly to occupy the rest of the Philippines. However, the defense of Bataan and the island had disrupted the Japanese timetable. Instead of taking fifty days to accomplish, as had been planned, Homma's troops had required 150.

JAPAN'S ADVANCE IN THE PACIFIC, JANUARY TO APRIL 1942 19

▶ United States Marines with full battle gear charge ashore for the assault on Guadalcanal Island in August 1942. Landing barges bring them to battle as part of the U.S. offensive in the Solomon Islands.

2 The Tide Turns in the Pacific, May to December 1942

KEY PEOPLE	KEY PLACES
🇯🇵 Admiral Isoroku Yamamoto	🇺🇸 Midway
🇯🇵 Admiral Osami Nagano	🇦🇺 New Guinea
🇺🇸 Admiral Chester Nimitz	🇦🇺 Solomon Islands
🇯🇵 Vice Admiral Nobutake Kondo	🇺🇸 Aleutian Islands
🇺🇸 Major General Alexander Vandegrift	🇬🇧 Guadalcanal

A new Japanese strategy in the Pacific began in spring 1942. The aim was to deliver a knockout blow to the U. S. Pacific Fleet before American industrial war production could make it too powerful.

There were disagreements, though. The debate centered on the place where the next wave should be. The Japanese Imperial Navy would play the dominant role in any further offensive, but was itself far from united. Admiral Isoroku Yamamoto, head of the combined fleet, wanted to copy Pearl Harbor in some form. Admiral Osami Nagano, head of the Naval General Staff, disagreed. He favored more island invasions. In the end, such indecisiveness would prove disastrous to Japanese plans.

Battle of the Coral Sea

Yamamoto believed that the U.S. Pacific Fleet, particularly the carriers that had escaped the attack on Pearl Harbor, were the greatest threat to Japan's security. He argued for a surprise thrust across the central Pacific to lure the U.S. into a fight against the Japanese combined fleet. Nagano suggested either a renewed push toward India and Ceylon or a drive into the southwest Pacific from Rabaul, New Britain, toward the island groups to the east of Australia and toward New Guinea and Papua.

The decision was made to go with a combination of Nagano's southwest Pacific drive and Yamamoto's plan. The small carrier *Shoho*, four cruisers, and a destroyer took troops to Tulagi on May 3. They then began to escort a larger force from Rabaul to Port Moresby. A second naval group, based on the two large carriers *Shokaku* and *Zuikaku* under Rear Admiral Takeo Takagi, was stationed east of the Solomons. Aircraft from *Yorktown* attacked Tulagi on May 4, but failed to halt the Japanese occupation of the island. The carrier then rejoined Task Force 17 in the central Coral Sea.

The U.S. suffered no losses in this first attack by American aircraft against an enemy carrier.

On May 7 Task Force 17 and elements of the Japanese fleet were steering westward across the Coral Sea on converging courses. The U.S. admiral sent his strike aircraft after two enemy carriers. The strike aircraft spotted the carrier *Shoho*, which was sunk after at least thirteen bomb hits and seven torpedo strikes. The U.S. suffered no losses in this first attack by American aircraft against an enemy carrier.

As *Shoho* came under attack, Japanese land-based aircraft from Rabaul attacked a U.S. squadron. Later, that squadron's force was mistaken for the enemy and attacked by U.S. bombers from Australia. Again it suffered no damage. At the same time, two destroyers, the *Sims* and *Neosho*, were hit by aircraft from Takagi's carrier force. The *Sims* succumbed quickly. However, the *Neosho* survived for four days until its burned-out hulk was sent to the bottom by a U.S. destroyer.

CARRIER WARFARE

Many traditionalists in World War II were slow to believe in the power of carriers. They still believed in big-gun battleships.

The Battle of Taranto in November 1940 demonstrated what carriers could do. Carriers and planes could accomplish victories, without the need for warships to come into close contact. Carriers could launch strikes from hundreds of miles away upon an unsuspecting target. Those strikes could inflict devastating damage at minimal cost. Although the Pacific War involved all types of warships, carriers became the most important. With its great industrial capacity, the United States was bound to win any race to build more and more aircraft carriers. Once available, the U.S. military could use them to reduce Japan's Pacific empire.

Carriers had several roles. First, they neutralized enemy warships, mostly at long range, in a purely naval battle. Therefore, the carriers needed early and accurate intelligence on the enemy's location, speed, and direction. Second, they supported amphibious assaults beyond the range of friendly land-based aircraft.

The deployment of carriers to support amphibious landings was complex. The carriers had to perform a variety of roles. To soften up a target island, aircraft from fast carrier task forces were deployed ahead of the main invasion fleet to strike at airfields and defensive installations. While these raids continued, an escort group of smaller carriers would sail with the invasion fleet to provide air cover. During the actual landings, carrier aircraft acted as flying artillery, aiding the naval bombardment of beaches.

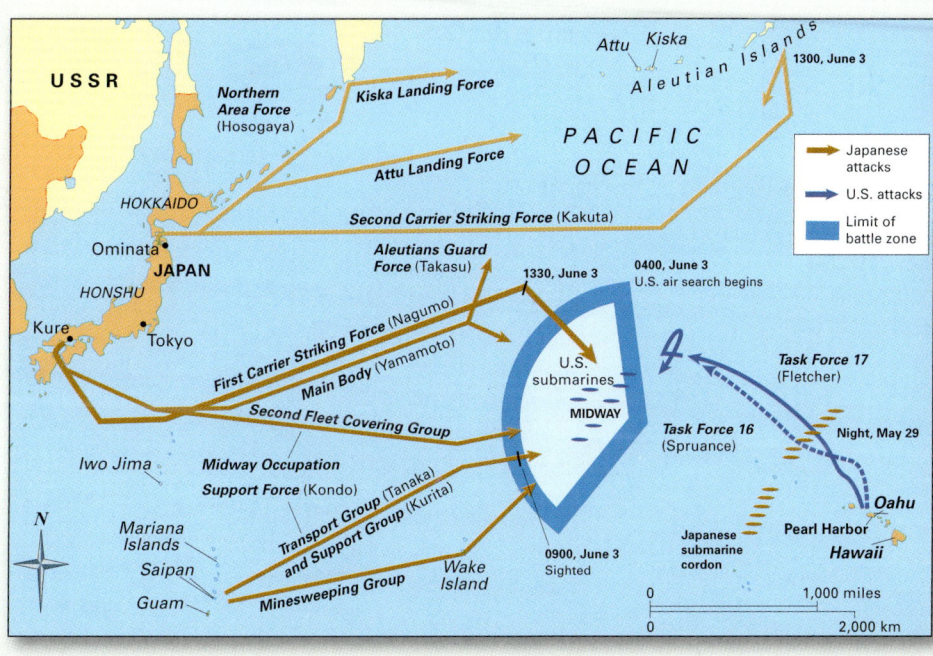

Victory at the Battle of Midway in June 1942 gave the United States naval parity with Japan.

THE TIDE TURNS IN THE PACIFIC, MAY TO DECEMBER 1942

The Japanese realized that the loss of *Shoho* left the invasion force without air cover. Takagi was ordered to move his carriers westward to provide protection. As they sailed, he also received information on the location of Task Force 17. Twenty-seven aircraft were to attack it at dusk. The U.S. was able to intercept them. Ten Japanese aircraft were shot down and a further eleven crashed into the sea while attempting to land. No U.S. aircraft were lost in the last action of the first day of the Battle of the Coral Sea.

Early on the morning of May 8 both sides launched strikes against each others' carriers. Although they had similar numbers of aircraft, the Japanese had better combat experience and torpedoes and their carriers were hidden under cloudy skies. Shortly before 11:00 p.m. aircraft from the *Yorktown* attacked *Shokaku*, but scored just two bomb and no torpedo hits. The pilots of the U.S. carrier *Lexington* managed only one bomb hit, but together, the damage was enough to force the carrier to withdraw to the island of Truk. The accompanying *Zuikaku* was never attacked.

The U.S. carrier *Lexington* was abandoned by its crew during the Battle of the Coral Sea. Not a single man was lost during the operation.

The Japanese arrived over Task Force 17 at around the same time. *Yorktown* suffered little damage from just one bomb strike. The *Lexington* appeared to survive as well, but it suffered damage when an electric spark ignited gasoline vapor from a ruptured fuel tank. Two hours later a second explosion caused severe fires that raged out of control. The crew abandoned ship. The U.S. destroyer *Phelps* sank the carrier with torpedoes.

The Battle of the Coral Sea was the first carrier battle. Both sides made several mistakes and both claimed victory. The Japanese called the battle a success because they had damaged Task Force 17's matériel. However, the U.S. achieved the greater and more important strategic victory. It had stopped the invasion of Port Moresby and undermined Nagano's plan.

> *The Battle of the Coral Sea was the first carrier battle. Both sides made several mistakes and both claimed victory.*

U.S. Victory at Midway

Believing that two U.S. carriers had been sunk at the Coral Sea, the Japanese attacked Midway, a tiny island some 1,100 miles (1,760 km) northwest of Pearl Harbor. They hoped to draw the remaining U.S. carriers into a large, costly battle. Yamamoto's plan was complex and involved most of the Combined Fleet, which was broken into separate task forces. The Northern Area Force was a diversionary force ordered to strike at the Aleutian Islands in the northern Pacific. Other forces were the Kiska and Attu Landing Forces and the Second Carrier Striking Force. On May 28 the Guard Force, the fourth part of the attack group, sailed with four battleships, two cruisers, and twelve destroyers. It was to be deployed between Pearl Harbor and the Aleutian Islands. Its aim was to intercept any U.S. ships sent to oppose the invasion of the islands.

> *Yamamoto's plan was complex and involved most of the Combined Fleet, which was broken into separate task forces.*

The attack on Midway involved several groups of warships. Vice Admiral Chuichi Nagumo's I Carrier Strike Force was to bomb the island early on June 4. This would pave the way for the landing of assault troops. It was hoped that the attack would draw the U.S. carriers into battle.

Yamamoto organized two other squadrons. The main body, three large battleships, including the *Yamato* and escorts, was to take up a central position between the Aleutians' Guard Force and the Midway Occupation Force under Vice Admiral Nobutake Kondo. A line of submarines was placed to the east of the island to warn of any U.S. approach.

> *The plan was ambitious and flawed.*

The plan was ambitious and flawed. First, although the Combined Fleet was much stronger than the U.S. Pacific Fleet, none of the groups could support the others. Second, I Carrier Strike Force lacked sufficient escort warships. At the same time, the battleship groups, which could have provided cover, lacked air cover of their own. Finally, and most importantly, the element of surprise did not exist due to U.S. code breaking.

Admiral Chester Nimitz, commander of the U.S. Pacific Fleet, sent a task force to the Aleutians. The air defenses of Midway were reinforced with the arrival of B-17 Flying Fortress bombers and fighters. Finally and crucially, a carrier task force was created at Pearl Harbor in late May. It was made up of *Enterprise, Hornet,* and *Yorktown*—the latter damaged at the Coral Sea but repaired in three days—twelve cruisers, fourteen destroyers, and nineteen submarines. The carriers took position and assembled north of Midway on June 1 undetected by the Japanese.

> *But Yamamoto's belief that attack would divert U. S. attention from Midway was mistaken.*

The attack on the Aleutians opened the battle on June 3. Japanese carrier-based aircraft raided Dutch Harbor. On June 6–7 the islands of Kiska and Attu were invaded—the only U.S. territory occupied during the war. But Yamamoto's belief that the attack would divert U.S. attention from Midway was mistaken.

The action around Midway also opened on June 3, when U.S. bombers and a torpedo plane damaged a tanker. At dawn next day Nagumo, stationed 180 miles (290 km) from Midway, sent around 50 percent of his carrier aircraft—108 planes—to bomb the island. The U.S. aircraft at Midway responded. Twenty-seven marine fighters met the raiders 30 miles (50 km) out at sea, but were outnumbered by the Japanese. Although able to shoot down fifteen enemy aircraft, they lost an equal number of fighters. Between 6:30 a.m. and 7:00 a.m. the Japanese destroyed a number of the island's installations but avoided the runways, since they expected to use them in the near future. Meanwhile the rest of Midway's aircraft attacked Nagumo's carriers. They did not inflict any damage and twenty U.S. aircraft were shot down.

The action around Midway also opened on June 3, when U. S. bombers and a torpedo plane damaged a tanker.

Meanwhile the rest of Midway's aircraft attacked Nagumo's carriers.

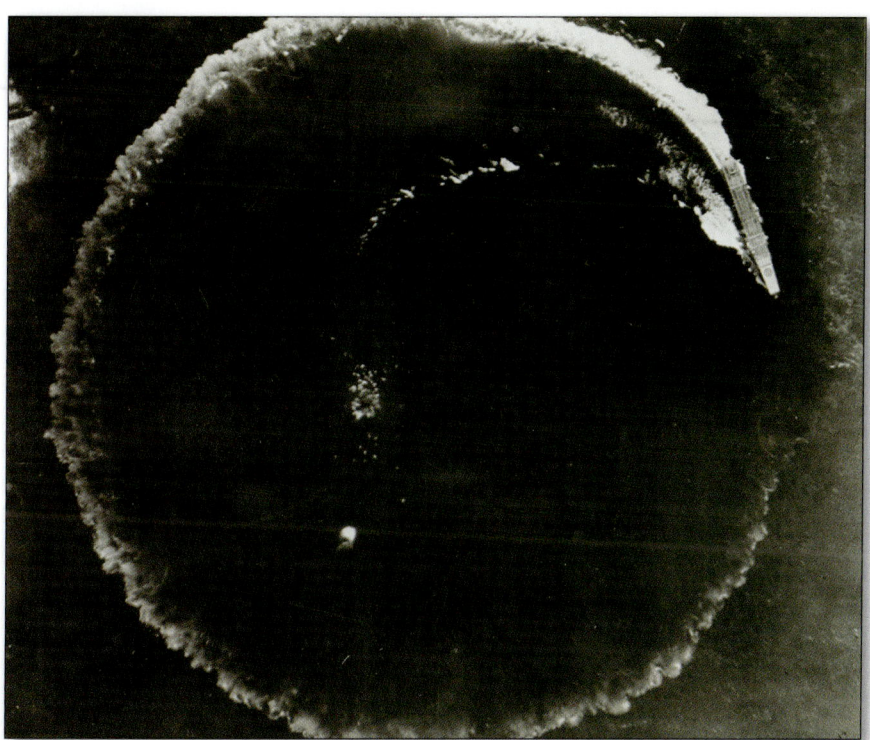

A Japanese carrier circles in the open sea to avoid an attack by U. S. planes. The aerial photograph was taken from a U. S. B–17 plane high above the battle of Midway.

THE TIDE TURNS IN THE PACIFIC, MAY TO DECEMBER 1942

EYEWITNESS

MITSUO FUCHIDA

Mitsuo Fuchida was a famous captain at the Battle of Midway in June 1942. He was on board the *Akagi* during the battle and recorded the carnage inflicted by U.S. bombers in a matter of five minutes.

> There was a huge hole in the flight deck behind the midship elevator. The elevator itself, twisted like molten glass, was dropping into the hangar. Deck plates reeled upward in grotesque configuration. Planes stood tail up, belching livid flame and jet-black smoke. Reluctant tears streamed down my cheeks as I watched the fires spread, and I was terrified at the prospect of induced explosions, which would surely doom the ship.

> I staggered down a ladder and into the ready room. It was already jammed with badly burned victims from the hangar deck. A new explosion was followed quickly by several more, each causing the bridge structure to tremble. Climbing back to the bridge, I could see that *Kaga* and *Soryu* had also been hit and were giving off heavy columns of black smoke. The scene was horrible to behold.

Extract from *Midway* by Mitsuo Fuchida and Masatake Okumiya, 1955.

The morning had gone well for the Japanese. Midway had been badly damaged and aircraft losses were light. At around 7:00 a.m. the *Enterprise* and *Hornet* launched their aircraft. These were followed thirty minutes later by half of *Yorktown*'s. Around 9:20 a.m. John Waldron, the commander of the *Hornet*'s torpedo bombers, spotted the enemy and attacked. The bombers scored no hits, and the Japanese fighters shot down all the planes, with only one man surviving. A second attack by torpedo bombers from *Enterprise* met a similar fate, with ten of fourteen aircraft destroyed. Again, the bombers recorded no hits.

> *The morning had gone well for the Japanese. Midway had been badly damaged and aircraft losses were light.*

Shortly after these attacks, dive-bomber squadrons from the *Hornet* and *Enterprise* arrived. The *Enterprise*'s bombers caught the Japanese by surprise. They scored several hits on the flight decks of the *Akagi* and *Kaga*. Both were set on fire. Then *Yorktown*'s torpedo and dive-bombers found the *Soryu* and scored several hits. By 10:25 a.m. three of Nagumo's carriers were in flames. *Kaga* and *Soryu* both sank that afternoon, while *Akagi* was abandoned and sunk by the Japanese two days later.

The position of *Yorktown* had been identified by a Japanese reconnaissance aircraft. But it did not detect the *Enterprise* and *Hornet*. Nagumo ordered the captain of his surviving carrier, *Hiryu*, to attack the *Yorktown*. They scored three bomb hits and forced it to reduce speed. A second strike occurred in the afternoon, this time by aircraft from the *Hiryu*. Mostly torpedo bombers, they arrived over *Yorktown* at 2:30 p.m. and scored two hits. The badly damaged carrier had to be abandoned about half an hour later. *Hiryu*'s success was short-lived. At 5:00 p.m. aircraft from *Enterprise* scored several hits, setting the carrier on fire and damaging its escorts. The *Hiryu*'s crew abandoned ship the following day. The carrier was then sunk by Japanese torpedoes.

> Then *Yorktown's torpedo and dive-bombers found the* Soryu *and scored several hits.*

The Japanese carrier *Akagi* was caught by a surprise attack. Several hits to the flight deck set it on fire. The Japanese sunk the ship with its own torpedoes two days later.

THE TIDE TURNS IN THE PACIFIC, MAY TO DECEMBER 1942

The loss of four carriers was a blow to Yamamoto. Still, he resolved to take one last gamble. He ordered Kondo's warships to seek out and destroy U.S. forces in a night action. It was a move expected by the U.S., which was already moving carriers beyond range of Kondo's ships. In the early hours of May 5, Yamamoto accepted that the U.S. carriers had escaped. He recalled Kondo, and pronounced the Midway operation ended.

The only U.S. vessels sunk during the Battle of Midway were lost during the final hours. Both fell victim to the Japanese submarine *I-168*. These losses were overshadowed by the disaster that had befallen the Japanese. Four large carriers had been sunk. All of their 275 aircraft were destroyed. Half of their crews had been killed, along with a further 3,500 naval personnel. Replacement carriers could not be built quickly or easily, nor could new crews be trained in a short time. Most serious was the loss of highly skilled veteran pilots. In contrast, U.S. manpower losses were comparatively small.

The victory at Midway gave the United States naval parity with the Japanese. For the moment, Japan had two large and three smaller carriers available, while the U.S. had three large ones. However, there were thirteen carriers close to completion in U.S. naval dockyards, while Japan had just six. Yamamoto's worst fears had been realized. The U.S. Pacific Fleet had survived Pearl Harbor and then Midway. The initiative in the Pacific had passed to the United States.

The Battle for the Solomons

There was debate among U.S. planners on what to do next. Admiral Ernest King, the newly appointed commander in chief of the navy, and General Douglas MacArthur both wanted to counterattack in the Bismarcks and

New Guinea area. But they disagreed over strategy. MacArthur wanted a direct attack by the U.S. Army on Rabaul. King favored "island-hopping" through the Solomons toward the same objective. The U. S. Joint Chiefs of Staff intervened. On July 2 they agreed to a three-stage operation along the lines proposed by King. Vice Admiral Robert Ghormley's South Pacific Area command was to recapture the southern Solomons, particularly Guadalcanal, where the Japanese were constructing an airstrip. MacArthur was to seize the interior and northern coast of New Guinea. Once these objectives had been achieved, Rabaul could be attacked from both the Solomons and New Guinea.

The U. S. Joint Chiefs of Staff intervened. On July 2 they agreed to a three-stage operation along the lines proposed by King.

MacArthur's New Guinea advance faced Japanese troops who had come inland on the north coast of Papua, headed for Port Moresby. Major

The USS *Missouri* saw action in the Pacific during the battles of Iwo Jima and Okinawa.

THE TIDE TURNS IN THE PACIFIC, MAY TO DECEMBER 1942 31

General Edmund Herring's Australian and U.S. troops finally halted the Japanese drive just 30 miles (50 km) from Port Moresby. Eventually they pushed the Japanese back, but the campaign delayed MacArthur's drive along the coast of New Guinea. Consequently, only the Guadalcanal element of the U.S. plan was put into effect.

Landings on Guadalcanal

The assault on Guadalcanal by Major General Alexander Vandegrift's U.S. 1st Marine Division on August 7, code-named Operation Watchtower, was the first U.S. offensive of the war. The opening phase went well. The neighboring islands of Tulagi fell on the first day. The Marines on Guadalcanal captured the developing Japanese air base, which was renamed Henderson Field. However, the Japanese response was swift. Intense air attacks and naval success forced the supporting supply ships and escorts and the protecting carrier task force to withdraw. The Marines were isolated and had little air cover until the first aircraft landed at Henderson Field on August 20.

Intense air attacks and naval success forced the supporting supply ships and escorts and the protecting carrier task force to withdraw.

A stalemate ensued. The Japanese tried to build up their strength by landing small numbers of troops under the cover of darkness. Darkness also allowed their warships to steam close to shore and bombard Henderson Field. U.S. naval and air forces dominated the daylight hours. At night they tried to halt the flow of Japanese supplies and their reinforcements.

The battle became known as the Battle of Bloody Ridge. Much of the fighting took place at night; the Marine line buckled but did not break.

The Japanese made two major attempts to crush the Marines. The first attempt, between September 12 and 14, was fought on high ground along the southern edge of the Henderson Field perimeter. The battle became known as the Battle of Bloody Ridge. Much of the fighting took place at night; the Marine line buckled but did not break. Finally, the Japanese retreated. The second attack followed in late October.

Between October 23 and 25 the U.S. perimeter was attacked, but the Japanese assaults suffered heavy losses. For six weeks, the U.S. command successfully skirmished with the Japanese while naval battles offshore continued. Vandegrift and the 1st Marine Division, exhausted and suffering from tropical illnesses, were withdrawn to Australia in early December. A new general, Alexander Patch, arrived. Heading a much larger force, he would oversee the final defeat of the Japanese on Guadalcanal in 1943.

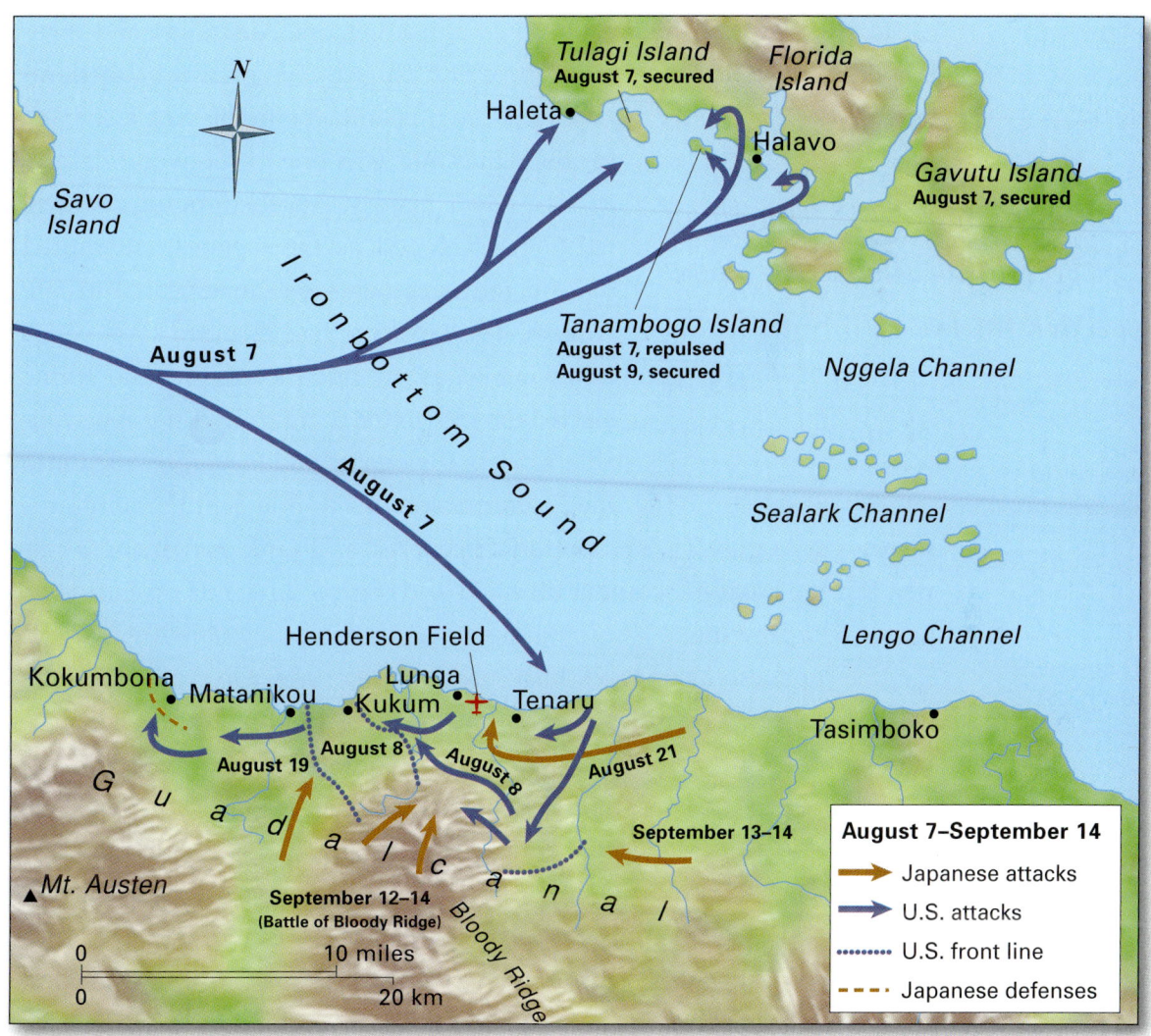

Operation Watchtower, the code name for the Guadalcanal campaign, began on August 7, 1942. The operation lasted six months and ended in defeat for the Japanese.

THE TIDE TURNS IN THE PACIFIC, MAY TO DECEMBER 1942 33

Naval Battles off Guadalcanal

Vandegrift's troops on Guadalcanal depended on air and naval forces to bring in ammunition, food, weapons, and troop replacements, and to take out battlefield casualties. The Japanese recognized that if they cut the supply lines, Vandegrift's troops would be isolated and probably defeated. Consequently, the waters off Guadalcanal became the focus of a naval campaign that lasted for six months. So many ships were lost that it gained the nickname "Ironbottom Sound."

In a totally one-sided action on August 8–9, one Australian and three U.S. cruisers were rapidly sunk and a fifth cruiser, *Chicago*, was badly damaged. Later known as the Battle of Savo Island, the battle was a setback for the Allies and was one of the worst defeats in U.S. naval history. Another round of naval fighting developed as the Japanese attempted to land reinforcements on Guadalcanal in late August. The Japanese had changed their codes following Midway, but increased radio traffic alerted the U.S. to the danger. Two of three available carriers, *Enterprise* and *Saratoga*, sailed into the Eastern Solomons to intercept the reinforcements. On August 24, U.S. aircraft discovered and sank one Japanese carrier. But the Japanese counter attacked and scored three hits on *Enterprise* before withdrawing.

Later known as the Battle of Savo Island, the battle was a setback for the Allies and was one of the worst defeats in U.S. naval history.

The Japanese also struck back using submarines. On August 31, the carrier *Saratoga* was put out of action for three months by the Japanese submarine *I-26*. On September 15 the *I-15* badly damaged the battleship *North Carolina*. After this the U.S. Navy had just one carrier, *Hornet*, and one battleship, *Washington*, fit for service in the Pacific.

Both sides then tried to land more of their troops on Guadalcanal. On October 11, U.S. transports and escorts made for the island, protected by a cruiser and destroyer squadron. At the same time Japanese transports and escorts were close by. The Japanese succeeded in sinking the U.S. destroyer *Duncan* and crippled the cruiser *Boise*. Two nights later, the battleships

Kongo and *Haruna* sailed into Guadalcanal unchallenged, and bombarded Henderson Field as Japanese troops were landed. This led to a change in U.S. command. Admiral William Halsey became commander of the South Pacific Area. Rear Admiral Thomas Kinkaid took command of the carriers *Hornet* and the hastily repaired *Enterprise*.

As Japanese land forces attempted to capture Henderson Field, Yamamoto ordered Kondo to destroy U.S. carriers. Halsey ordered Kinkaid to destroy Kondo's force of two large and two small carriers. Both launched strikes on October 26. U.S. aircraft damaged the small *Zuiho* and the larger *Shokaku*. The *Enterprise* was badly damaged, and the *Hornet* was abandoned and eventually sunk by a Japanese destroyer. The Battle of Santa Cruz Islands was a clear Japanese victory. However, it came at the cost of one hundred aircraft and experienced pilots.

The U.S. battleship *North Carolina*, shown here in heavy seas, was one of many ships damaged during the fight to control Guadalcanal.

THE TIDE TURNS IN THE PACIFIC, MAY TO DECEMBER 1942

CHESTER NIMITZ

KEY FIGURES

Admiral Chester Nimitz (1885–1966) was the outstanding U.S. commander of the Pacific War. He was responsible, along with Admiral Ernest King, for devising the strategy of "island hopping."

Immediately after Pearl Harbor, Nimitz was promoted to admiral. Made commander of the U.S. Pacific Fleet, in March 1942 he was in charge of all air, land, and sea forces in the theater. Nimitz's main area of responsibility was the central Pacific. Here he directed a series of amphibious operations against Japanese-held islands, beginning with the Gilberts in November 1943 and ending with the occupation of Okinawa in 1945.

Nimitz was a superb manager, able to smooth over dissent. He also gathered senior commanders capable of carrying out his plans with skill. Perhaps his greatest attribute was seeing the importance of carrier-based air power in the Pacific.

Admiral Chester Nimitz

Between November 12 and 15, as both sides tried to land reinforcements, there were a series of battles known as the Naval Battle of Guadalcanal. On the night of November 12–13, action in "Ironbottom Sound" produced heavy losses on both sides. But a U.S. squadron prevented enemy reinforcements landing on the island. Some Japanese troops reached Guadalcanal on the following day, but between November 14 and 15, two U.S. battleships, *Washington* and *South Dakota*, met a Japanese flotilla in "Ironbottom Sound." *Washington* wrecked both the battlecruiser *Kirishima* and a destroyer, forcing the Japanese to retreat.

The naval battle convinced the Japanese that U.S. forces on Guadalcanal could not be defeated. The Japanese began to develop new defenses across the Central Solomons. Those Japanese troops remaining on Guadalcanal received a trickle of supplies to delay any U.S. drive into the new zone. Under cover of darkness on November 30, eight destroyers packed with supplies were led into "Ironbottom Sound." A U.S. squadron intercepted them off Tassafaronga Point and in the opening exchange sank one Japanese destroyer. The Japanese executed a fighting withdrawal. They first steamed toward Wright, then fired several Long Lance torpedoes, before retreating northward. One U.S. cruiser was sunk and three others damaged, but no supplies reached Guadalcanal.

The naval battle convinced the Japanese that U.S. forces on Guadalcanal could not be defeated.

This widespread series of naval engagements helped to decide the battle for Guadalcanal. None of the engagements were decisive; however, together they helped to shape the outcome. The contest had matched Japan's fewer warships and highly experienced sailors against the greater numbers of the United States Navy. The campaign became one of attrition, swapping loss for loss. This kind of exchange was a process that the U.S. Navy could better endure. The seabed of "Ironbottom Sound" was littered with wrecks from both sides. Because the U. S. had a strong industrial base and was more able than the Japanese to make up for its maritime losses, the United States was better able to survive. Guadalcanal was a turning point in the Pacific War. This victory for the United States became a springboard for more successes.

▶ Chinese workers await supplies dropped from planes overhead during the building of the Burma Road.

3 Burma and China, 1942 to 1943

KEY PEOPLE	KEY PLACES
🇯🇵 General Shijiro Iida	🇲🇲 Burma
🇬🇧 Lieutenant General Harold Alexander	🇲🇲 Lashio, Burma
🇬🇧 Major General William Slim	🇹🇼 Yunnan, China
🇺🇸 General Joseph Stilwell	🇲🇲 Rangoon, Burma
🇹🇼 Jiang Jieshi	🇵🇭 Arakan, Philippines
🇺🇸 Colonel Claire Chennault	

The capture of British-controlled Burma (now Myanmar) interested the Japanese for several reasons. Its location made it a good place from which to protect the resources of the southwest Pacific. Or it could be used to launch attacks into India. Its capture would also seal the Burma Road, which ran from northern Burma into southwestern China. The Chinese nationalists relied on the Burma Road for transporting the supplies that they needed to oppose the Japanese. Finally, Burma was a good source of oil and rubber, both wartime assets.

The British did not think Burma would be a major Japanese target. As a result, few regular British army units supported the local forces and border guards. The British had many other commitments on the home front and in the Middle East. They were also involved in the campaigns in the Pacific.

On December 21, 1941, evidence of the danger to Burma became clear. Neighboring independent Siam (Thailand) signed a treaty with the Japanese against the Allies. Its terms gave Siam parts of Burma, Malaya, (Malaysia) and Indochina (Vietnam, Laos, and Cambodia) in exchange for letting the Japanese station troops and build air bases there.

Invasion of Burma

The Japanese advance into Burma from Siam opened on January 12, 1942. Units of General Shijiro Iida's Fifteenth Army pushed across the border toward Tavoy and Moulmein. Iida's army was joined by troops from Malaya and a group of Japanese-trained Burmese nationalists, the Thirty Comrades, led by Aung San. Some 4,000 Burmese sided with the Japanese.

The Burma Corps, under Lieutenant General Thomas Hutton, was made up of weak, poorly-equipped, and isolated British, Burmese, and Indian troops. Despite their efforts, the capital city of Moulmein (now Mawlamyaing) fell at the end of the month. The British retreated behind the Salween River to form a new line of defense. Iida crossed the river at Paan, north of the new line, forcing Hutton to retreat behind the Sittang River. After a bitter five-day battle at Bilin in February, the British blew up the only bridge in the area to prevent the Japanese from crossing. Unfortunately, this action left half of the British troops on the wrong side. Most of them eventually crossed but left behind weapons and equipment.

Alexander realized that his forces were tired and demoralized. Their total collapse seemed imminent.

Despite the destruction of the bridge, the Japanese crossed the Sittang and advanced toward the capital, Rangoon (now Yangon). The British received reinforcements and a new commander, Lieutenant General Harold Alexander, on March 5. Alexander realized that his forces were tired and demoralized. Their total collapse seemed imminent.

Two days later, Alexander ordered a withdrawal to the north. He wanted to defend a new line in central Burma. He was helped by 30,000 Chinese soldiers of the Fifth and Sixth Armies. They supported nationalist leader Jiang Jieshi and were led by Jiang's U.S. military adviser, Lieutenant General Joseph Stilwell. Now commanded by Major General William Slim, the Burma Corps positioned itself to cover the Irrawaddy River valley. The Chinese Fifth Army held Toungoo to cover the Sittang River and links between Rangoon and Mandalay. The Sixth Army covered the mountainous jungle region between the Sittang and Salween rivers.

Japanese efforts to pierce the line began on March 21. Iida struck the Chinese Fifth Army at Toungoo. The Fifth staged a fighting withdrawal to the north along the Rangoon–Mandalay railroad. The main Japanese blows fell against the British and the Chinese Sixth Army. From April 10 to 19, the British forces fought stubbornly to retain control of Magwe and the oil field around Yenangyuang. However, they were pushed back as the Japanese trapped one of the British divisions while destroying the oil field. The blow against the Sixth Army began on April 18 when Japanese troops from the 56th Division overwhelmed the Chinese at Loikaw. They then struck northward toward Lashio, the southern end of the Burma Road.

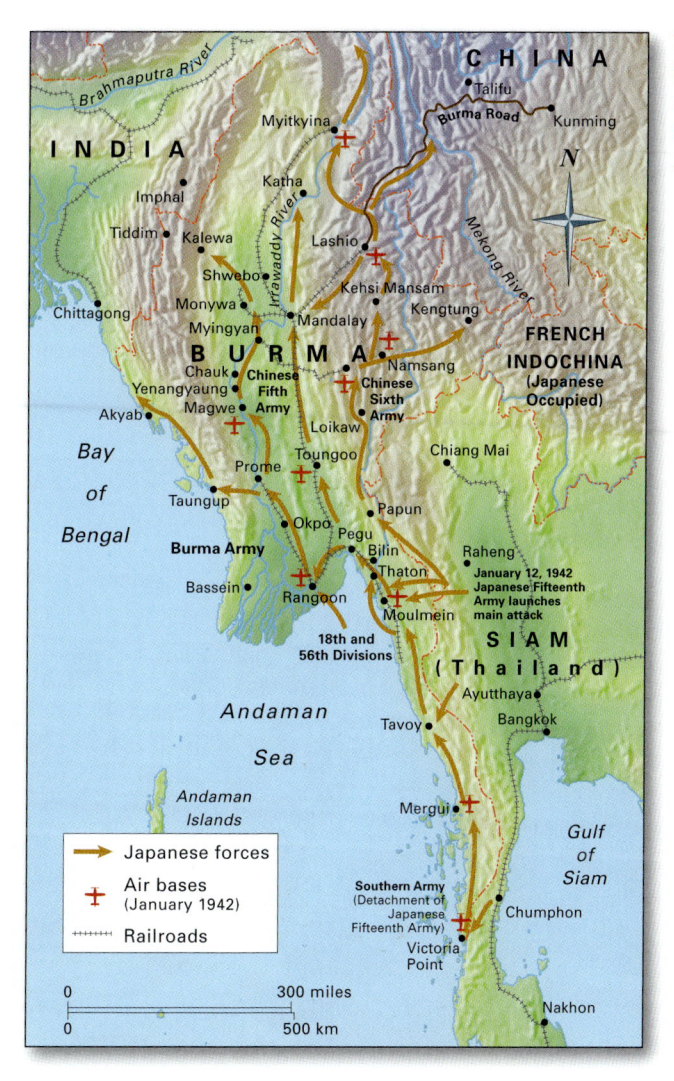

The Japanese invaded Burma from neighboring Siam (Thailand) on January 12, 1942.

British Retreat to India

Lashio fell on April 29. The 56th Division turned south toward Mandalay intending to block any retreat by Alexander and Stilwell's remaining forces. Both Allied commanders recognized that southern and eastern Burma had been lost. They ordered their forces to retreat across the Irrawaddy River by the only available bridge. The evacuation was completed late on April 30.

Alexander and Stilwell retreated northward on different routes. The British, with Slim's Burma Corps fighting a series of skillful actions, retreated along the Chindwin River toward Tiddim in the west. There, a single track led over the mountainous border to northeast India. The withdrawal was completed by May 11. British casualties were enormous. Just one-third out of 36,000 men completed the 900-mile (1,450-km) retreat from Burma, the longest in British military history. Most of the survivors were exhausted and sick, and morale was low. The Japanese called off their pursuit along the line of the Chindwin. Both sides settled down to ride out the heavy rains of the monsoon season.

> *Just one-third out of 36,000 men completed the 900-mile (1,450-km) retreat from Burma, the longest in British military history.*

Japanese troops enter Mandalay on May 1, 1942. With Mandalay secured, the Japanese gained control of central and northern Burma.

KEY FIGURES

JOSEPH STILWELL

General Joseph Stilwell (1883–1946) was the commander of U.S. and Chinese forces in the China-Burma-India theater of operations. He had difficult relationships with the British and Chinese. This earned him the nickname "Vinegar Joe."

Stilwell, a fluent Chinese speaker, was appointed military adviser to Jiang Jieshi, leader of the Chinese Nationalists, shortly after Pearl Harbor. He took charge of the Chinese forces opposing the Japanese in Burma in 1942. He later held several positions at the same time, including as Jiang's adviser and deputy to Britain's Lord Louis Mountbatten, the Allied supreme commander in Southeast Asia. The roles demanded military and political skills.

Stilwell often had bitter arguments with his allies. Yet he remained true to the goal and proved a reliable supporter of both the British and Chinese in day-to-day fighting. Although he admired the courage and actions of the Chinese soldiers, his relationship with Jiang deteriorated. As a result, Stilwell was recalled to Washington at Jiang's insistence in March 1944. His replacement was Major General Albert Wedemeyer.

General Joseph Stilwell

KEY FIGURES

THE FLYING TIGERS

The Flying Tigers were a group of U.S. pilots. Their goal was to keep the Burma Road supply route to China open in late 1941 and the first half of 1942.

The unit gained its nickname because its fighters, P-40 Kittyhawks, had their engine air intakes painted with fanged jaws in black, red, and white. Its official name, however, was the American Volunteer Group (AVG). It consisted of some one hundred P-40s bought by China from a U.S. manufacturer, and volunteer pilots from the United States. The AVG was formed in 1941 by Colonel Claire Chennault, the U.S. aviation adviser to Chinese Nationalist leader Jiang Jieshi.

With British permission, the squadrons trained in Burma beginning in July. On December 10 Jiang ordered the group's 3rd Squadron to transfer to an air base near Rangoon to combat the Japanese invasion. Jiang sent the rest of the AVG to Kunming, Yunnan Province, in southwest China. There they would protect supply shipments moving along the Burma Road. By mid-February 1942 the P-40s had shot down one hundred enemy aircraft, losing just fifteen of their own. Pilots received $500 for each victory.

But the Japanese advanced through southern Burma and closed on Rangoon. The 3rd Squadron was ordered to move to central Burma. Then it was sent back to Kunming in May. In July the Flying Tiger squadrons were incorporated into the United States Army Air Force and became part of the U.S. China Air Task Force. During their independent career, the AVG had shot down 299 Japanese aircraft and damaged 300 more.

The vibrantly painted noses of P-40 Kittyhawks gave them the name of "Flying Tigers."

44 HORRIFIC INVASIONS

The Chinese troops were repeatedly split up by Japanese attacks, but they managed to fight their way to safety and to assist the British retreat to India. Despite these successes, the Chinese were badly hurt in the campaign. Japanese casualties totaled just 7,000 men, and the Japanese ended up in control of 80 percent of Burma.

Stilwell's surviving forces were split into several groups by the Japanese advance. Half retreated to the northeast, crossed the border back into China, and re-formed in Yunnan. Two divisions retreated through northern Burma. One of them ended up in India and the other trekked to Yunnan by way of southern Tibet. The 38th fought its way westward, crossed the Chindwin River, and reached Imphal on May 24. Stilwell also escaped and set up headquarters in Delhi, India.

Japanese Naval Raids

As the fight for Burma continued, on March 23, 1942, the Imperial Japanese Navy began attacks in the Indian Ocean. First it set its sights on Ceylon (Sri Lanka), home to a major British naval base. The Japanese admirals also sought to carry out raids into the Bay of Bengal, a vital shipping lane. The fleet in Ceylon was commanded by Vice Admiral Nobutake Kondo and had five aircraft carriers, four battleships, and eleven other warships. Vice Admiral Jisaburo Ozawa led the Bay of Bengal-bound fleet, which consisted of the light carrier *Ryujo* and fourteen escort ships. Reports of these raids alarmed the British. Japanese success in the Indian Ocean could be a stepping stone into the Persian Gulf and Red Sea. Then Japanese forces might join with German forces in North Africa.

To combat the threat, the British established the Far Eastern Fleet under Admiral James Somerville. He commanded three carriers, five battleships, and more than thirty other warships. However, several of his warships dated from World War I. Also, Somerville's one

> *Reports of these raids alarmed the British. Japanese success in the Indian Ocean could be a stepping stone into the Persian Gulf and Red Sea. Then Japanese forces might link up with German forces in North Africa.*

hundred aircraft were outnumbered by superior Japanese planes. On the morning of April 5, the *Cornwall* and *Devonshire* were spotted off Ceylon and attacked by eighty Japanese aircraft from Kondo's fleet. Most scored hits and faced only light antiaircraft fire. Both cruisers sank rapidly. Four days later, *Hermes*, the world's oldest carrier (launched in 1919), and the Australian destroyer *Vampire* were sunk shortly after leaving Ceylon.

These setbacks forced the British to withdraw to East Africa. As result, the Japanese had free reign in the Indian Ocean. However, both Kondo and Ozawa withdrew on April 8, returning to the Pacific to prepare for operations in the southern Solomons. Their departure marked the end of the only major Japanese incursion into the Indian Ocean.

New Allied Strategies Emerge

After the retreat from Burma in 1942, the Allies needed to open a new supply route to China. The loss of the Burma Road made it likely that Jiang could be starved of supplies. Such an outcome would free one million Japanese troops for service elsewhere in the Pacific and East Asia. This possibility alarmed both Britain and the United States. Stilwell, now commanding general of the China-Burma-India theater, began to develop a new supply link. This link flew to China from northeast India by way of the eastern Himalayas in southern Tibet. The terrain over which the aircraft flew was so mountainous that it was nicknamed "the Hump" by the U.S. pilots.

At first, however, there were few transport aircraft available. As a result, Stilwell also began planning a new land route into Yunnan from northeast India by way of northern Burma. He used the Chinese units in India for the drive into northern Burma. U.S. military advisers helped retrain the troops. Reinforcements and supplies were flown from northeast India over the Hump, and new equipment was brought in. All of these preparations took time. Stilwell saw that opening his new route would have to take place when the dry season began in October 1942. Privately he believed that it could not be finished until late 1943.

At the same time, General Archibald Wavell, the new British commander, began strengthening India's border defenses. He created a new

THE CHINDITS

STRATEGY & TACTICS

The Chindits were British, Indian, and Nepalese units used in two deep raids in Burma during early 1943 and 1944. The name comes from the Chinthe, a mythical Burmese lion.

The idea was the brainchild of Brigadier Orde Wingate, an officer with experience in unconventional warfare. He believed that "long-range penetration" based on speedy movement would catch the Japanese off guard. On the first raid his aim was to launch hit-and-run attacks against communications links deep inside enemy territory. On the second mission, he established bases in Japanese territory and then attacked Japanese rail links.

Neither operation was very successful. Casualties were high, including Wingate, who was killed in an air crash during the second raid. After he was killed, the British army did not train any more units for this type of operation.

The First Arakan campaign and the Chindit raids did not change the situation in Burma. But it did convince Wavell that his troops could not undertake large-scale operations until the dry season of 1944 to 1945. However, the relative failure of the missions led to command changes. Wavell, recently promoted to field marshal, accepted the position of viceroy of India. General Claude Auchinleck took Wavell's role. Lord Louis Mountbatten became the Allied supreme commander of the Southeast Asia Command area. The new Fourteenth Army, under General William Slim, would conduct future operations in Burma.

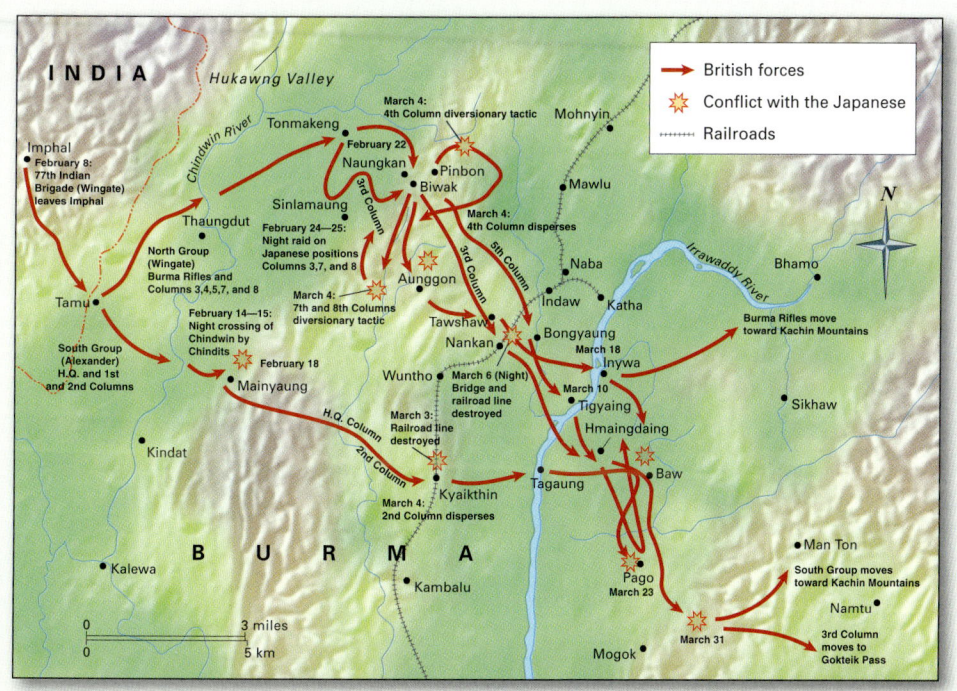

The first Chindit operation took place in February 1943, when 3,000 troops penetrated deep behind Japanese lines in Burma.

Anglo-Indian Army to oppose a Japanese invasion. Like Stilwell, he knew his forces were too weak to retake Burma for at least a year. He also knew that his troops felt outclassed by the Japanese soldiers, who seemed to be almost superhuman jungle fighters. Wavell planned two campaigns to regain the initiative and to restore the morale of his command.

First Arakan Offensive

The first of Wavell's attacks was directed from India into Arakan. Arakan is in northwest Burma, isolated from the rest of the country by mountainous jungle. The operation, which would attack Japanese airfields, was conducted by the 14th Indian Division. It began in December 1942. The division pushed southward from the border through the province. The Japanese built a defensive line around the town of Akyab. The British suffered se-

The Arakan Offensive began in December 1942 as the first British operation against the Japanese in Burma. The offensive ended in failure, unfortunately, when the Japanese counterattacks forced the British to withdraw in May 1943.

48 HORRIFIC INVASIONS

vere casualties trying to break through between January and March of 1943. General Iida ordered his 55th Division to advance from Akyab. He also ordered other units to strike though the province's border mountains.

Between March 13 and 17, the Japanese attacks nearly crushed the 14th Division, which retreated into India, leaving behind most of its supplies. The five-month First Arakan Offensive was a failure and confirmed the Japanese soldier's excellence at jungle warfare. Arakan also proved that the British were still too weak to carry out offensive operations.

Stilwell and the Burma Road

In February 1943 Stilwell responded to a Japanese thrust against his attempts to build a road to the border. The Chinese 38th Division threw them back into Burma. Stilwell chose to conduct his own operation to reopen the Burma Road.

Stilwell's troops moved out in October, the beginning of the dry season. By mid-November they were pushing down the Hukawng Valley. The Japanese surrounded parts of the 38th Division. The arrival of Stilwell encouraged the Chinese to resume their attack in late December. They were able to secure part of the valley by the end of the year. More fighting would be needed before the road was completely rebuilt.

China's Continuing Crises

Meanwhile, Jiang's forces in China were weak. In a series of minor Japanese "rice offensives" in China, the Japanese seized food. Also, air supplies were diverted from the Chinese to Chennault's U.S. Fourteenth Air Force.

Chennault's continuing successes in the air war over China was at first due to the volume of supplies he was receiving. Stilwell wanted them directed to the Chinese forces in Yunnan. Jiang Jieshi became involved. Their arguments led to restrictions on the Flying Tigers' air operations.

By the end of 1943 the Allied position in Burma, China, and India was not promising. The Japanese hold on both Burma and China seemed firm. The link between India and China was still poor. The Allies were starved of men and resources, and their leaders were divided.

▶ British prime minister Winston Churchill and U.S. president Franklin D. Roosevelt at Casablanca, Morocco, in January 1943.

4 War in the Pacific, 1943

KEY PEOPLE	KEY PLACES
🇺🇸 Vice Admiral William Halsey	🇦🇺 Rabaul
🇺🇸 Admiral Chester Nimitz	🇦🇺 New Georgia
🇺🇸 Vice Admiral Raymond Spruance	🇦🇺 Bougainville
🇯🇵 Vice Admiral Jinichi Kosaka	🇦🇺 New Guinea

The British and U.S. had agreed at the Casablanca Conference in January 1943 to defeat Germany before Japan. Still, U.S. industry was producing great amounts of arms and equipment. Arms not needed in the Atlantic or in Europe were diverted to the Pacific. Therefore, larger U.S. offensives could be undertaken there.

At the beginning of 1943, the two main areas of combat in the Pacific were the islands of New Guinea and Guadalcanal, both in the southwest. In the far north the Japanese held two U.S. islands within the Aleutian Islands. With greater resources available, Admiral Chester Nimitz, the commander in chief of the U.S. fleet in the Pacific, wanted to open a new front in the central Pacific.

U.S. victory on Guadalcanal in February 1943 and the weakness of Japanese forces in New Guinea led the Japanese to reevaluate their strategy. They chose to base their defenses on Rabaul, on New Britain in the Bismarck Islands. Rabaul offered excellent docking facilities, and aircraft based there could fly over the whole theater of operations.

Beyond Rabaul, the Japanese strengthened their garrisons in the central Solomons and off the northeast coast of New Guinea. The Imperial Navy's vice-admiral Jinichi Kosaka was in control of the entire region. The defense of the Solomons, however, was the responsibility of General Haruyoshi Hyakutake's Seventeenth Army. New Guinea was held by the Eighteenth Army under Lieutenant General Hotaze Adachi.

Japanese ground forces were scattered across these areas. The Japanese hoped that each group could hold back invaders long enough for aircraft and warships based on Rabaul to counterattack. They also tried to disrupt the Allied buildup on Guadalcanal and New Guinea by launching an air offensive. Between April 7 and 16, some 400 aircraft struck across the southwest Pacific. Their pilots made inflated claims of success. These exaggerations led Admiral Isoroku Yamamoto, head of the Combined Fleet, to visit airfields in the northern Solomons. U.S. intelligence discovered details of his trip through its Magic code-breaking operation. On April 18 long-range fighters were sent from Guadalcanal to intercept his flight over Bougainville. The admiral was killed in the attack. Japan thus lost of one of its most skilled commanders at a time of crisis.

The admiral was killed in the attack. Japan thus lost of one of its most skilled commanders at a time of crisis.

Clearing Southern New Guinea

The U.S. recognized the importance of Rabaul. Initially, a two-pronged advance, code-named Operation Cartwheel, was planned to take it. One prong would move along southern New Guinea. The other would move from the southern Solomons. They would join together to attack New Britain. They were to be commanded by General Douglas MacArthur and Admiral William Halsey.

MacArthur's forces planned to advance northward along the coast in a series of leapfrogging amphibious assaults. They would be led by General Walter Krueger's U.S. Sixth Army and backed by Australian forces. If successful, each would get them closer to the west coast of New Britain.

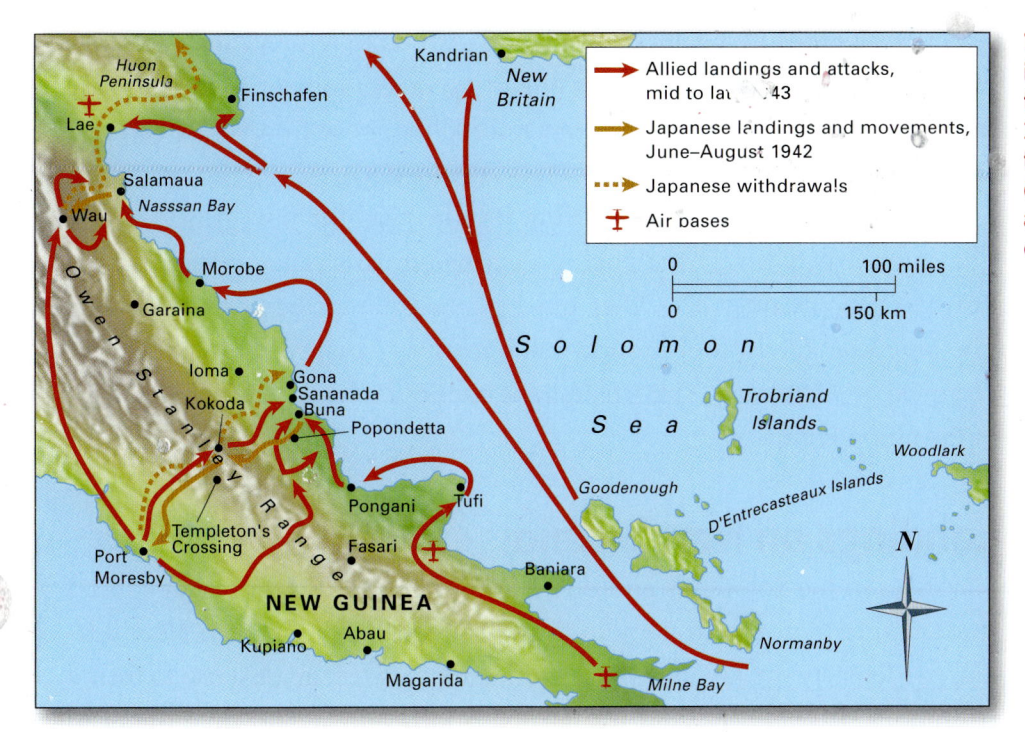

The Allied campaign in New Guinea and the Solomon Sea in 1943 showed that the U.S. strategy was determined to gain air superiority and to control the seas.

MacArthur had two large naval task forces to support Krueger. A third group, Lieutenant General George Kenney's Fifth Air Force, was to hit distant Japanese bases. It was also to gain air superiority over any target, support ground operations, and transport men and supplies.

The importance of Kenney's Fifth Air Force was proven at the Battle of the Bismarck Sea in early 1943. On February 28 a Japanese convoy carrying 7,000 men and escorted by eight destroyers was sent to Lae on New Guinea's east coast. On March 2 the convoy was intercepted by Kenney's bombers. Despite poor weather over the following days, all of the transports and half of the escorts were sunk. The remaining destroyers limped back to Rabaul with serious damage.

In late June, the Allies launched a drive to capture Lae. By the end of August, Australian and U.S. troops advanced on the town from east and west. On September 4 the Australian 9th Division came ashore from U.S. landing craft. In four days they advanced to within 5 miles (8 km) of Lae. Meanwhile, U.S. paratroopers had dropped onto the airfield at Nadzab to the west on September 5.

WAR IN THE PACIFIC, 1943

By September 14 the 7th Division had pushed to within 7 miles (10 km) of Lae. The two Australian forces linked up on September 16 to complete the occupation of the town. However, 6,000 Japanese troops had escaped and retreated to the mountainous Huon Peninsula.

That area, directly opposite New Britain, was the next Allied target. The chief objective was the port of Finschafen. Australian troops landed nearby on September 22. Other units pushed along the coast from Lae. The Japanese garrison of around 5,000 men was ousted. Finschafen was occupied on October 2. The Australians continued to push along the coast of the Huon Peninsula.

Landings on New Britain

Successes in the Solomons and on New Guinea by late September caused leaders to rethink the strategy in the southwest Pacific theater. New Britain, particularly the Japanese base of Rabaul, was still an obstacle to future operations. It was protected by 100,000 troops and would be difficult to capture. Thus, the decision was not to wage a long battle for the island. Instead, it would be isolated from outside help, encircled by U.S.-held islands and naval forces, and subjected to air attack. At the same time, the push deeper into the Japanese-held Pacific would continue. Nevertheless, MacArthur argued that western New Britain and its airfields needed to be captured.

The main force, the U.S. 1st Marine Division, landed on the north coast on December 26. They would battle until May 1944.

The Allies had taken Lae and Finschafen. They had also won bases from which an amphibious assault could be launched. MacArthur quickly made use his advantage. As the Australians continued to root out the scattered Japanese on the Huon, he ordered an assault on western New Britain. The main force, the U.S. 1st Marine Division, landed on the north coast on December 26. They would battle until May 1944. But the Marines secured two key airfields within a few days of landing. They steadily drove the Japanese from the island's west over the following months.

Clearing the Central Solomons

The second strand of Operation Cartwheel was the island-hopping drive from Guadalcanal by way of New Georgia and Bougainville in the northern Solomons to New Britain. Halsey's tasks were to develop the South Pacific Area forces into the Third Fleet and to establish the Third Amphibious Force. Some operations against the Japanese took place during this time. Operation Cleanslate, the capture of the Russell Islands north of Guadalcanal by the U.S. 43rd Infantry Division, began on February 11. It was concluded without a fight. The Japanese garrisons had been evacuated. Construction work on airfields, harbor facilities, and a radar site began. Landings of 6,000 men on Rendova off the southwest coast of New Georgia on June 29–30 were another important step. The next phase, called Operation Toenails because it provided artillery positions to protect the island, was the invasion of New Georgia itself.

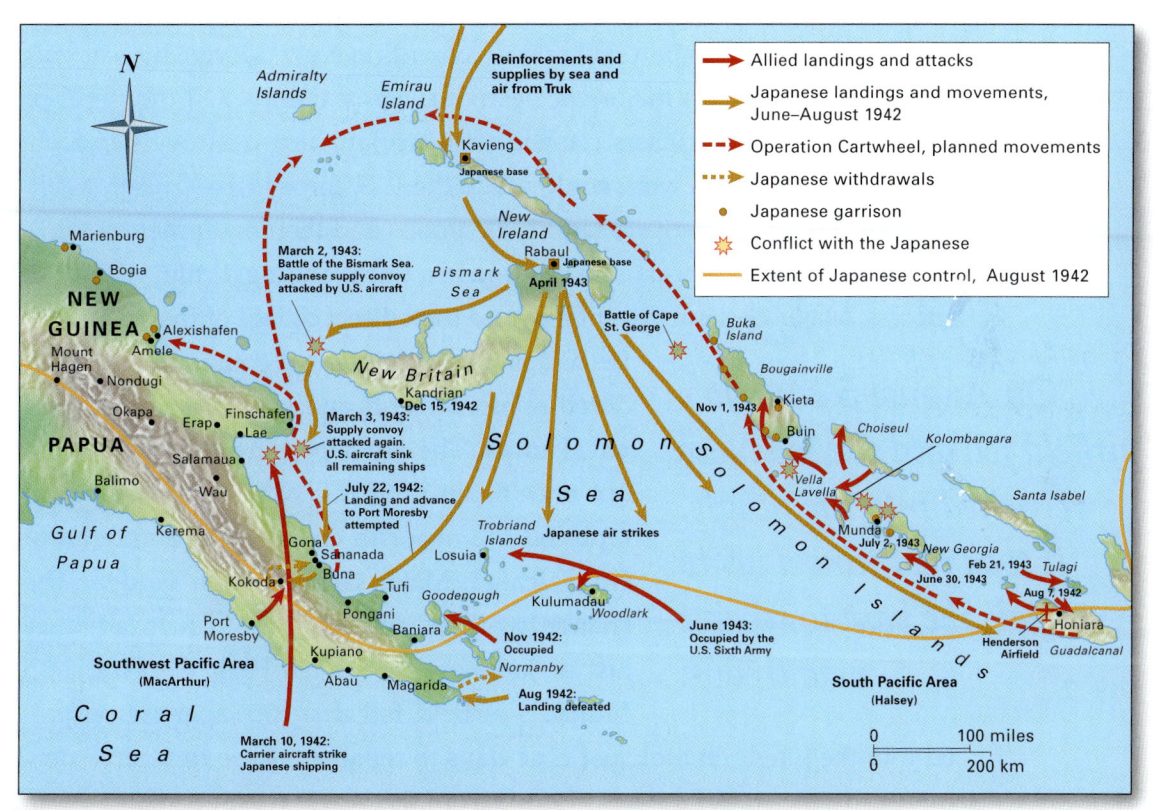

The plan for Operation Cartwheel was a two-part advance from southern New Guinea and from the southern Solomons that was to end in an attack on New Britain.

WAR IN THE PACIFIC, 1943   55

New Georgia was the main support of the new Japanese defensive line across the central Solomons. It was held by 10,000 troops. New Georgia's main town, Munda, on the southwest coast, had a valuable airfield. The U.S. made the decision to land because the force could be protected by aircraft from Guadalcanal. Also the capture of Munda's airfield would help the island-hopping advance.

> *Almost immediately, difficult jungle terrain, intense tropical heat, and Japanese resistance combined with a lack of experience to stall the advance.*

The main landings on New Georgia began July 2. One division came ashore 5 miles (8 km) northeast of Munda. They met little opposition. Three days later a smaller U.S. force landed at Rice on the north shore. These troops sought to isolate Munda. The others struck toward the town and its airfield. Almost immediately, difficult jungle terrain, intense tropical heat, and Japanese resistance combined with a lack of experience to stall the advance. Japan sent reinforcements to New Georgia by sea. This effort resulted in two major clashes with U.S. warships. On the night of July 5–6, U.S. light cruisers clashed with ten Japanese destroyers in Kula Gulf. Two destroyers were sunk, while the U.S. force lost a cruiser. Later, the Japanese did manage to land 2,000 troops and their equipment.

Back on New Georgia, the U.S. made a third landing. It met with little success. Major General Oscar Griswold took direct charge of the operation. He had just been appointed commander. He ordered reinforcements and support from air and naval units. The advance renewed on July 25, but once again progress was limited. Griswold replaced the major in charge with a veteran of Guadalcanal, Major General John Hodge. The change worked, and troops began to advance just as Japanese troops fell back. On August 5 Munda's airfield fell and the Japanese retreated into the jungle. It took just nine days to repair the base to receive new troops. By the end of the month the rest of the island was secured.

> *On August 5 Munda's airfield fell and the Japanese retreated into the jungle. It took just nine days to repair the base to receive new troops.*

WILLIAM HALSEY

KEY FIGURES

Vice Admiral William Halsey (1882–1959) was a senior U.S. naval figure in the Pacific. He was a hard-driving commander, determined to seek out and destroy the enemy. Halsey's strategy for using carriers, which he described as "hit hard, hit fast, and hit often," proved remarkably successful in crippling the Imperial Japanese Navy.

Halsey took part in many important U.S. operations of the Pacific War, beginning with raids on occupied islands. He was promoted to command the South Pacific Area and oversaw the defeat of the Japanese naval forces off Guadalcanal. This victory eventually led to the isolation of the major Japanese base at Rabaul by the end of 1943.

Halsey was criticized for his action off Luzon in October 1944. It nearly led to a successful Japanese surprise attack on his escort carriers. He was also censured for losing ships in a tropical storm. He later took charge of the final stages of the Okinawa campaign and launched raids against the Japanese home islands in the final months of the war.

Vice Admiral William Halsey (on left)

WAR IN THE PACIFIC, 1943

New Georgia had cost the U.S. 1,000 men killed and four times as many wounded. The Japanese recorded around 10,000 casualties. They now hoped to hold on to their last island in the northern Solomons, Bougainville, as long as possible. The Japanese assumed that the U.S. intended to attack their principal base Rabaul on New Britain. But in late August the U.S. Joint Chiefs of Staff decided to bypass Rabaul. New Britain was to be isolated. Still, Bougainville and other islands to its south had to be captured first.

This engagement marked the end of the successful U.S. campaign to clear the central Solomons. Halsey turned his attention to the north.

Halsey opted to bypass Kolombangara, immediately north of New Georgia, and land on Vella Lavella. At dawn on August 15, a United States' regiment hit the beaches on the south coast. It met little resistance. The Japanese made no attempts to bring in reinforcements. The few defenders there were hunted down over the following weeks. By the end of September the island's airfield was in operation. The remaining Japanese troops were withdrawn on September 6. This engagement marked the end of the successful U.S. campaign to clear the central Solomons. Halsey turned his attention to the north.

The Battle for the Northern Solomons

After the capture of Vella Lavella, Bougainville was the last main Japanese position of significance north of New Britain. The Japanese garrison on Bougainville was made up of 60,000 troops. They were mostly in the north and south of the island, leaving the center lightly defended. Halsey selected units from Alexander Vandegrift's I Amphibious Corps to land on the north shore of Empress Augusta Bay. The area was defended by just 300 Japanese soldiers when the 3rd Marine Division came ashore on November 1. The Japanese launched attacks using Rabaul-based aircraft and a naval squadron. On the night of November 1–2 the Battle of Empress Augusta Bay saw Japanese warships intercepted by four cruisers and eight destroyers. Japan lost a cruiser and a destroyer and withdrew.

On November 5, aircraft from the *Saratoga* and *Princeton* scored several hits on the Imperial Navy. Six warships were badly damaged and the strike was called off. Six days later the carriers *Bunker Hill*, *Essex*, and *Independence* launched aircraft against Rabaul, causing severe damage. These victories ensured that U.S. forces could continue to Bougainville without interruption. The Japanese on the island were isolated.

JOHN F. KENNEDY

KEY FIGURES

Lieutenant John F. Kennedy (1917–1963) commanded the U. S. torpedo boat PT109, when it was rammed and sunk on a nighttime operation in the Solomons. The collision between the Japanese destroyer *Amagiri* and the PT109 killed two crew members and badly injured others. As the boat sank, Kennedy ordered his men to head for Plum Pudding Island. For two nights, Kennedy and one of his crew swam far out into Ferguson Passage to attract the attention of any searching U.S. PT boats. When that failed, the group swam to Olosana Island. From there, Kennedy and a crewmember made for Naru, on the northern part of Ferguson Passage. Here they found food and a canoe left behind by the Japanese. They used the canoe to try to reach the base at Rendova.

Although their attempts to get to Rendova failed, two Australian coastwatching scouts spotted their injured crew. The scouts informed the U. S. authorities at Rendova. Kennedy, who had traveled by canoe to Kolombangara to meet the island's chief coastwatcher, was the first to be picked up. He and the other surviving crew members returned to Rendova on August 8, seven days after setting out on the mission.

Lt. Kennedy's dramatic rescue attempts were important messages in his future campaign to become president of the United States. He won the 1960 election in a victory for the Democratic Party.

John F. Kennedy

WAR IN THE PACIFIC, 1943   59

On Bougainville, the 37th Infantry Division arrived on November 8. Within days U.S. strength on the island totaled 34,000 men. The Japanese moved through dense jungle to assault the U.S. forces in November and December. They suffered heavy casualties and made no progress. Attempts by the Japanese navy to prevent the U.S. buildup also failed. On November 25, destroyers sank three enemy destroyers. The U.S. engineers then constructed three airfields. They also developed Empress Augusta Bay into a major naval base by the end of the year.

Attempts by the Japanese navy to prevent the U. S. buildup also failed.

The Gilberts Liberated

Admiral Chester Nimitz also pursued a course in the central Pacific, the second axis of the proposed drive toward Japan. To undertake this task, Nimitz assembled vast armadas of ships. Chief among Nimitz's resources by the fall of 1943 was the Fast Carrier Task Force. It was made up of twelve carriers with 800 aircraft under Vice Admiral Raymond Spruance, and naval formations, later known as the Fifth Fleet. Nimitz also organized the Fifth Amphibious Force to transport and protect U.S. Army and Marine units that would carry out amphibious assaults.

Many of these new units had never taken part in amphibious operations on a large scale. Others had never even seen combat. Still, Nimitz thought it was time to put the theory of amphibious warfare into practice.

The objectives he chose were Makin and Tarawa, small coral-reef-fringed atolls 100 miles (160 km) apart in the Gilberts. The Gilberts were British-controlled islands occupied by the Japanese since December 1941. U.S. Marines had successfully raided Makin in August 1942 to destroy a radio station. The Japanese later reinforced the main garrison on Betio and the main island of Tarawa, and strengthened its defenses. By late 1943, 2,600 troops and 2,000 Korean construction workers were on Tarawa. Extensive defenses had been constructed, many

By late 1943, 2,600 troops and 2,000 Korean construction workers were on Tarawa.

60 HORRIFIC INVASIONS

TARAWA

STRATEGY & TACTICS

The U.S. landed on Tarawa, the main island of the Gilberts, on November 20, 1943. Tarawa was the first classic amphibious assault of the Pacific campaign. Tarawa became a testing ground for tactics adopted in the 1930s by the U.S. Navy and Marine Corps. The U.S. forces in the operation, code-named Operation Galvanic, lacked combat experience. The few specialized weapons and equipment available, such as tracked landing craft, were new.

The attack on Tarawa itself had several problems. Japanese defenses had not been taken out by U. S. air and naval bombardments. The covering fire from nearby warships was almost halted during the landings, allowing the Japanese to man their weapons. Communications between the air, land, and sea forces were poor.

All of these issues were later addressed so that more troops could be landed simultaneously. Many new amtracs (amphibious tractors) were equipped with machine guns and heavier weapons. The crews of some warships, mainly older cruisers and destroyers, trained on the Hawaiian island of Kahoolawe to provide gunfire support. Their accuracy improved and bombardments became longer and heavier. Existing radios were waterproofed and provided with more batteries. Specialized command ships, usually transports converted to carry communications equipment, were produced.

Aside from these developments, the troops at the "sharp end" received better training and equipment to deal with enemy defenses. There were more machine guns and flame throwers, as well as demolition charges. The coordination of tanks and infantry was improved, too.

Operation Galvanic was a bitter lesson. The U.S. public called it "bloody Tarawa" because of the high casualties. But it was a learning experience for the U.S. military and prepared the public for the trials to come.

hidden. The island bristled with fifty artillery pieces, several light tanks, and machine guns. The Japanese planned to hold this island for as long as they could, as well.

The Gilberts were chosen as a target in summer 1943 because they would make ideal air bases for the capture of the Marshall Islands. The invasion, code-named Operation Galvanic, was scheduled for November 21. For seven days before the assault, both Makin and Tarawa faced air attack from land-based bombers and aircraft from Spruance's Fast Carrier Task Force. Then they were pounded by warships.

The softening up process seemed to have worked on Makin, which was defended by 350 enemy troops and a few hundred Korean laborers. The reinforced 27th Infantry Division stormed ashore. They took just three days to secure the island. Nevertheless, some 500 Japanese were killed. Just 100 surrendered. U.S. losses totaled sixty-six killed and 152 wounded on land. A Japanese submarine torpedoed and sunk an escort carrier, *Liscombe Bay,* killing 640 of its crew.

> *The reinforced 27th Infantry Division stormed ashore. They took just three days to secure the island.*

U.S. Marines on Tarawa in the Gilbert Islands suffered a shockingly high number of casualties, forcing changes in amphibious assault tactics.

The 2nd Marine Division landed on Tarawa on November 20. Major General Julian Smith, veteran of the latter stages of the Guadalcanal campaign, commanded the forces. As they approached the atoll in their tracked amphibious landing craft, the pre-assault land and air bombardment seemed to have silenced the enemy. The first wave landed at around 9:00 a.m. Soldiers took cover behind a 4-foot (1.2-m) seawall built from coconut logs. Later waves were far less fortunate. Their larger landing craft stuck on the coral atoll. Soldiers had to wade ashore through waist-high water in the face of intense Japanese fire. U.S. warships and aircraft could not reply for fear of hitting their own men.

The Marines already on Tarawa were not faring much better. Many were pinned down behind the seawall. Those who made it over the top found themselves fighting an often unseen enemy. One Marine commander, Colonel David Shoup, saw the chaos and mounting casualties and signaled: "Issue in doubt." Night fell. Fires from burning fuel drums illuminated the scene and helped deter a Japanese counterattack.

Five hundred troops charged the Marine lines. Many were cut down by naval fire, howitzers, and machine guns. The remainder were killed in close combat.

On November 21 the Marines, aided by reinforcements and howitzers, pushed inland and pounded the Japanese bunkers at point-blank range. The third day brought further progress but then the Japanese counterattacked. Five hundred troops charged the Marine lines. Many were cut down by naval fire, howitzers, and machine guns. The remainder were killed in close combat. The Tarawa group of islands was declared secure at 1:12 a.m. on November 23. Marine losses on the main island of Betio were 1,000 killed and 2,000 wounded—high for a three-day battle.

The heavy casualties at Tarawa and the willingness of the Japanese to fight to the death shocked the U.S. public. The press eulogized the bravery of the Marines. The operation highlighted weaknesses in amphibious warfare, however. The commanders learned important lessons for the landings on the Marshall Islands in February 1944.

KEY EVENTS

THE MAGIC CODE BREAKERS

A highly secret code-breaking operation, known as Magic, gave the U.S. advance warning of Japanese intentions in the Pacific. Magic allowed the U.S. to meet any new threat.

Magic was set up in 1939 as a means of breaking Japanese diplomatic and military codes. The chief aim was to break the so-called Purple code, created on a complex cipher machine. The breakthrough came in September 1940, when an army cryptologist, Colonel William Friedman, succeeded in breaking Purple, but ruined his health. The Purple code success was a great leap forward, but the operation was slowed by personnel shortages, lack of cooperation between departments, and the time still needed to decipher the messages. These all combined to produce its greatest failure—the lack of forewarning of the Pearl Harbor attack.

By 1942 matters had improved greatly. The department, made up of the navy's Communication Security Unit and the army's Signal Intelligence Service, employed hundreds of personnel. It decoded a huge number of messages. U.S. planners were given reports on Japan's activities almost as soon as they were received. This allowed them to prepare for their decisive victory at Midway—the turning point of the Pacific War.

Actions in the Aleutians

In June 1942 the Japanese had occupied two islands in the U.S. Aleutians, Attu and Kiska. The U. S. was determined to retake them . . .

Although the southwest and central Pacific were the key theaters of the Pacific War, the Arctic north was also important. In June 1942 the Japanese had occupied two islands in the U.S. Aleutians, Attu and Kiska. The U. S. was determined to retake them as a point of national pride rather than a strategic necessity. The Japanese had already given up thoughts of using the Aleutians to launch attacks on the United States. But small Japanese garrisons still fortified the two islands. They relied on aircraft flying from Paramushiro and naval forces for supplies and additional protection. The main U.S. base in the area was at Dutch Harbor on Umnak.

64 HORRIFIC INVASIONS

Attempts to isolate Attu and Kiska further began in early 1943. On March 26 a squadron of U.S warships, under the command of Rear Admiral Charles McMorris, were operating at the southern entrance to the Bering Sea. The warships clashed with Japanese cruisers and destroyers that were moving supplies to Attu. The Battle of the Komandorski Islands opened with a long-range gunnery duel that left the main U.S. warship, the heavy cruiser *Salt Lake City*, and the Japanese cruiser *Nachi* badly damaged. A U.S. torpedo attack from McMorris's destroyers drove off the remaining Japanese warships. Komandorski ended Japanese attempts to use surface vessels to resupply the Aleutians. The Japanese used submarines instead.

With Attu and Kiska now more isolated, the Allies decided to retake the islands. An amphibious task force, under the command of Admiral Thomas Kinkaid, landed the 12,000-strong 7th Infantry Division on Attu on May 11, under a cover of thick fog. It took the division eighteen days to neutralize the enemy. Fighting in biting winds and cold, the men of the 7th Infantry Division had to destroy bunkers and other fortifications. They were finally able to raise the U.S. flag over Attu on May 28. In the battles, only twenty-nine Japanese soldiers were captured out of the 2,500-strong garrison. The rest either died in combat or committed suicide. Allied losses totaled 561 dead and approximately 1,130 wounded. The island of Kiska was occupied without casualties in a joint Canadian–U. S. operation on August 15. In that operation, the Japanese troops in the garrison had slipped away undetected at the end of July.

The Aleutians were now back under U.S. control. Forces remained there for the rest of the war. They carried out bombing raids on mainland Japan. They patrolled the north Pacific, and they also acted as a diversion. The obvious intent of the diversionary tactics was to make the Japanese believe that the Aleutian Islands might be the springboard for a full-scale U.S. invasion of their Japanese homeland.

> *Fighting in biting winds and cold, the men of the 7th Infantry Division had to destroy bunkers and other fortifications. They were finally able to raise the U.S. flag over Attu on May 28.*

▶ Soviet troops attack through German barbed-wire entanglements, May 1943. Ultimately, the Soviets would push the Germans all the way back to Berlin.

5. The Tide Turns in Eastern Europe, 1942 to 1943

KEY PEOPLE	KEY PLACES
Adolf Hitler	Stalingrad, Russia
General Erich von Manstein	Leningrad, Russia
General Georgi Zhukov	Caucasus
General Vasily Chuikov	
General Friedrich von Paulus	
Field Marshal Wilhelm List	

In December 1941, German forces were thrown back from near Moscow. This event was a result of Red Army counterattacks along the eastern front. The German military was caught by surprise. They were mostly unprepared for the bitter cold. Joseph Goebbels, the Nazi propaganda minister, asked the German public to donate warm clothing to the troops fighting on the eastern front. This lack of planning cost the German soldiers dearly as they struggled to contain the Soviet advances. The Red Army's advances were halted only in the north, near Finland and around Leningrad (now St. Petersburg).

Leningrad Endures

Leningrad had been under siege since August 1941. Only the arrival of General Georgi Zhukov on September 12 saved the city from capture. Leningrad was under constant aerial attack by the Luftwaffe and was short of supplies. But the city managed to endure. This survival was thanks to its determined defenders, the high morale of its citizens, and the supplies that were arriving over the frozen Lake Ladoga. However, German and Finnish attacks threatened this supply lifeline. So Leningrad's population starved. Thousands died from cold, illness, and hunger. Significant relief did not arrive until January 1944—nearly 900 days after the siege began.

Germany's Summer Offensive

The Russian winter offensive had great success elsewhere in 1941 to 1942, with profound consequences for the German army. Furious at the failure of his generals, Hitler fired many of them by late 1942. He made himself supreme commander on December 19.

Hitler was obsessed with the idea of creating *lebensraum* (living space) for the German people in the east. He was also firmly committed to crushing Communism. So Hitler planned a summer offensive for 1942. He transferred divisions from the Balkans and western Europe to the eastern front.

PARTISAN WARFARE

STRATEGY & TACTICS

During 1942 and 1943, bands of Russian partisans, or civilians, fought the Germans from behind enemy lines. Their efforts supported the Red Army.

These partisan bands were set up shortly after the German invasion of 1941. In the beginning there were problems with organization, arms, and communication. By 1942, these problems were solved. The partisans concentrated on slowing the movement of supplies to the German front line. So, the partisans attacked isolated posts, bridges and railroads.

In response, the Germans deployed 250,000 men to guide their supply and communications line. They hunted down the partisans in a brutal campaign of terror. Despite these actions, the partisans continued their attacks until they were liberated by the Red Army.

68 HORRIFIC INVASIONS

However, these reinforcements were not the mobile infantry divisions. The eastern front needed all types of divisions as they waited for new recruits to be trained. Germany's Axis partners, chiefly Hungary, Italy, and Romania, did provide more units. However, they were not as well trained as the German units. Fewer troops were in each division and they lacked training and modern weapons.

The existing German armored divisions received better equipment. They got more powerful tanks, troop transports, and artillery. However, they were limited by a growing shortage of fuel. The Luftwaffe was feeling the strain of all-out war. When several fighter units were transferred to the western European theater, the German ground support bombers were left unprotected.

> *The Luftwaffe was feeling the strain of all-out war.*

Capture of Sevastopol

At the beginning of May the weather began to improve. Hitler had a plan for another offensive. This plan focused on the southern part of the eastern front. All available forces were concentrated in the Ukraine for a three-stage offensive.

First, the Germans planned to smash Red Army units along the Don River. Next, they would overtake Stalingrad (now Volgograd), an important industrial and communications center. Last, they would overrun the oil fields in the Caucasus. In the plan, code-named Operation Blue, Field Marshal Feodor von Bock commanded the Army Group South, which was split into two groups: Army Group A and Army Group B. However, before the main operation could begin, the remaining parts of the Crimean Peninsula still held by the Red Army had to be captured. The Eleventh Army, part of Army Group A, was chosen for this task.

On May 8, 1942, General Erich von Manstein's Eleventh Army, began the drive through Crimea. Soon it forced the Russian forces outside Sevastopol to retreat and then withdraw. Sevastopol, the major Soviet port on the Black Sea, was under siege on July 7. But its defenders were determined. The Soviets forced the Germans to fight for every inch of territory.

Only the loss of high ground overlooking the port sealed its fate. The campaign ended on July 11, 1942. The Germans took a total of 95,000 Soviet prisoners. General von Manstein was promoted to field marshal.

Meanwhile, the Red Army, led by Marshal Semyon Timoshenko launched an offensive attack against the Sixth Army around the city of Kharkov. The Sixth Army, part of Army Group B, was commanded by General Friedrich von Paulus. The initial Soviet attack gained ground, but the Germans launched a counterstrike. Red Army troops, forbidden by Stalin to retreat, were encircled. They surrendered on May 28. Army Group South took 214,000 prisoners. The Germans lost approximately 20,000 men.

> *The initial Soviet attack gained ground, but the Germans launched a counterstrike. Red Army troops, forbidden by Stalin to retreat, were encircled. They surrendered on May 28.*

The Sixth Army continued to push eastward. They crossed the Donetz River and established positions to strike at Stalingrad. The first stage of Operation Blue, the push toward the Don River, began on June 28. Progress was rapid—30,000 Soviet troops surrendered at Voronezh in early July. On the 15th German troops marched into Millerovo, a town halfway to Stalingrad. This early success prompted Hitler to redirect some of Army Group B forces. These forces would support Army Group A attacks on Rostov. This transfer of forces left Paulus's Sixth Army as the only force headed for Stalingrad.

Hitler's Fatal Intervention

On July 23 news of the capture of Rostov lifted Hitler's spirits. He drew up new and controversial objectives for his forces. Rather than concentrating against Stalingrad first and then turning to the Caucasus, he ordered a simultaneous attack. To make matters worse, Hitler ordered the transfer of top-grade divisions away from the two army groups. This left the less able Hungarian, Italian, and Romanian units to hold the front lines. Rather than concentrating force on a single objective, Hitler expected fewer troops to take on multiple missions.

The Battle for Stalingrad

The commander of Army Group B, Field Marshal Maximilian von Weichs, knew that his forces were stretched thin. He could rely on only one formation, the German Sixth Army under General von Paulus, to carry out the attack. His other units protected the flanks of the advance. The attack began in late July. Progress was initially slow because of a shortage of armored units and stiff Russian resistance. By late August–early September, German units reached the west bank of the Volga River to the north and south of Stalingrad. The vast industrial city, covering a narrow strip of land that stretched 20 miles (32 km) along the river's western bank, was isolated. Its garrison, the Sixty-second Army under Lieutenant General Vasily Chuikov, could only receive reinforcements by ferries from the east bank.

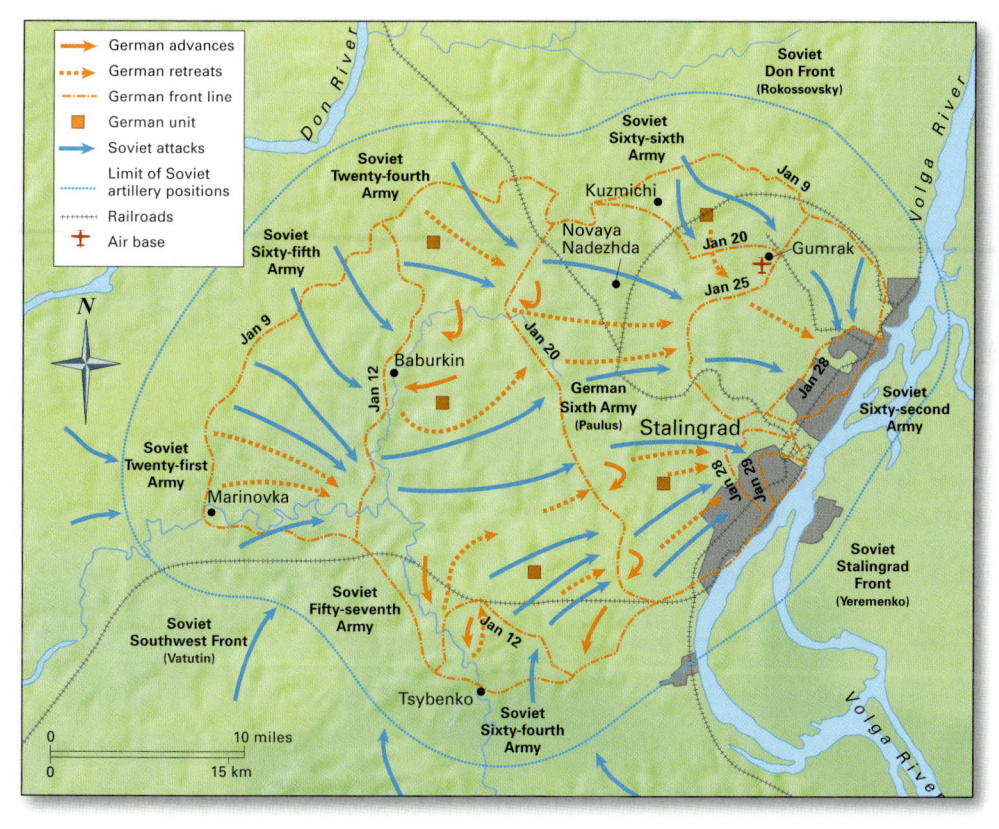

The long and bitter struggle by Soviet forces to recapture the city of Stalingrad was code-named Uranus. The struggle began on November 18, 1942. It finally ended on January 30, 1943, with the surrender of German Field Marshal Friedrich von Paulus.

THE TIDE TURNS IN EASTERN EUROPE, 1942 TO 1943

General von Paulus believed that the defending troops were weak and had poor morale. He decided to attack immediately. He was probably unaware that on July 28 Stalin had forbidden further retreats.

By late September, the new Russian resolve was apparent to German soldiers and their commanders. Chuikov based his defenses on the city's modern buildings, particularly its factories. Their concrete construction offered good protection against many types of artillery. German infantry units were forced to fight without support from tanks. In addition, the streets of Stalingrad were largely covered in piles of rubble, much of it produced by Luftwaffe bombing, making them impassable.

The push into the Caucasus by German Army Group A, commanded by Field Marshal Wilhelm List, was also stalling. The troops were exhausted, fuel was scarce, and much of their equipment failed. Promised reinforcements did not arrive. To make matters worse, List's two main armies were advancing independently, one southward to the Black Sea coast and the other southeastward to the Caspian Sea. The further they moved, the more separated they became. The growing lack of progress infuriated Hitler, who fired List on September 9. Hitler took personal command of Army Group A's operations. He did little to improve matters. No major reinforcements reached the tired troops. German attacks ground to a halt on the lower slopes of the Caucasus Mountains.

General Georgi Zhukov persuaded Stalin to launch a massive counterattack around Stalingrad in order to isolate General von Paulus's Sixth Army. On November 19 in the attack code-named Operation Uranus, the Red Army attacked to the north of Stalingrad.

> *...the Red Army attacked to the north of Stalingrad. Using a combination of heavy artillery bombardment followed by armored and cavalry units, the Soviet forces smashed through opposing troops.*

Using a combination of heavy artillery bombardment followed by armored and cavalry units, the Soviet forces smashed through opposing troops. A day later, Red Army units launched the second prong of the encirclement. Again, Romanian forces gave way, and the Soviet troops pushed northwestward. The two great wings of the Red Army offensive linked up on November 23, isolating the Sixth Army.

VASILY CHUIKOV

KEY FIGURES

Vasily Chuikov (1900–1982) was a Soviet general renowned for his skillful defense of Stalingrad between September and November 1942. He and his army later went on to spearhead the final push to the Berlin in 1945.

Before commanding the defense of Stalingrad, Chuikov had considerable military experience. Between 1926 and 1937 he was an adviser to Chinese nationalist leader Jiang Jieshi. In 1940 he took part in the Russian occupation of eastern Poland and had seen action in the Russo-Finnish War. He was appointed commander of the Sixty-second Army in May 1942. It became the mainstay of the Stalingrad garrison.

Chuikov reorganized the city's defense. House-to-house and street-to-street fighting steadily exhausted the attackers. This effective strategy allowed the Russians to retain a small part of Stalingrad along the western bank of the Volga River. Both psychologically and practically, the defense plan was decisive. Russian morale and confidence rose, while the Germans were left vulnerable to a successful Russian counterattack.

Vasily Chuikov

Hitler dismissed all thoughts of retreat. He ordered Paulus to stand fast and await the arrival of a relief force. The worn-out Sixth Army commander responded: "Our ammunition and petrol supplies are running out. Several batteries and antitank units have none left. Supplies not expected to reach them in time."

Hermann Göring convinced Hitler that German aircraft, under General von Manstein, could fly in enough supplies to preserve the Sixth Army. The counterattack opened December 10 and drove forward quickly. Within eight days the advance army group was only 30 miles (48 km) from Stalingrad. Yet the Red Army attacked to isolate the garrison further and widen the gap.

The Red Army's Operation Saturn opened on December 16 and was chiefly directed against the Italian Eighth Army and the Romanian Third Army. Both collapsed rapidly. General von Manstein ordered the unit nearest Stalingrad to withdraw to avoid encirclement. Vital airfields used in the faltering German resupply effort also fell to the Red Army. The German forces at Stalingrad were more isolated than ever.

> *The worn-out Sixth Army commander responded: "Our ammunition and petrol supplies are running out. Several batteries and antitank units have none left. Supplies not expected to reach them in time."*

The Sixth Army Surrenders

By January 1943 Stalingrad was a lost cause, although Hitler would not accept the realitiy of the situation. Hungarian and Italian troops holding the line east of Kharkov were close to collapse. Other units were falling back from the oil fields of the Caucasus to avoid encirclement by Russian forces. Confirmation of the mounting crisis came on February 6, when General von Paulus and the Sixth Army surrendered at Stalingrad.

On January 9, 1943 General von Paulus refused Russian surrender terms. Within a week a massed infantry and tank assault had overrun two-thirds of the German-held pocket. It captured the airfield at Gumrak, where aircraft had been bringing in supplies and taking out the wounded. The end was in sight, and on January 22 Paulus sent a message to Hitler, which hinted that surrender was the only real option.

Hitler refused to consider defeat. The Russian attacks continued. On January 26 the German pocket was split in two. As the Axis divisional commanders began to surrender steadily, General von Paulus was promoted to field marshal by Hitler on January 29. The implication was clear—the Sixth Army commander was expected to commit suicide rather than surrender, since no German officer of that rank had ever surrendered. Nevertheless, Paulus and Russian officials and agreed to surrender terms.

The Sixth Army was destroyed during the battle for Stalingrad. About 200,000 German and other Axis troops were killed before the surrender on January 30. Paulus led into captivity 94,000 of his troops—ill, weak, starved. Few would live to return home. Huge quantities of weapons and equipment had been destroyed or captured around Stalingrad. Field Marshal von Paulus's surrender was seen as an act of betrayal by Hitler, who raged against his commander's failure to take his own life.

Manstein's Masterstroke at Kharkov

As the battle for Stalingrad entered its final phase, the Russian troops continued to push westward. Huge tank forces quickly overran Kharkov and drove toward the great bend in the Dnieper River. The strategic position was critical. Hitler turned to one of his most able generals, Field Marshal von Manstein, to stabilize the southern eastern front.

On February 21 Army Group South unleashed its counter-offensive toward Kharkov. The German forces were outnumbered around seven-to-one. Spearheaded by three elite Waffen SS divisions, the Germans smashed though General Nikolai Vatutin's Southwest Front. The gap in the Russian line allowed the attack on Kharkov, which fell a month later on March 14.

The recapture of Kharkov came not a moment too soon. Within a few days the spring thaw turned the roads to mud and brought a halt to further operations. Field Marshal von Manstein's victory at Kharkov was remarkable. The Russians recorded 50,000 dead and 20,000 taken prisoner. The victory temporarily boosted the flagging German morale.

The victory propaganda for Kharkov ignored the true strategic position on the eastern front. The city's recapture did not compensate for the disaster at Stalingrad or the loss of most of the territory won in the summer of 1942. Retaking Kharov was a limited effort to stabilize a dangerous situation. The reality was that by spring 1943 Germany no longer had the resources, men, or equipment to win battles. The German army and its Axis partners had suffered almost 1 million casualties in the previous twelve months. The Red Army had also lost as many casualties. Unlike the Soviet Union, the Germans did not have extra soldiers to make up the losses.

In 1943 the Soviets overran the city of Kharkov. The German counterattack in February and March of 1943 retook Kharkov and stabilized the eastern front.

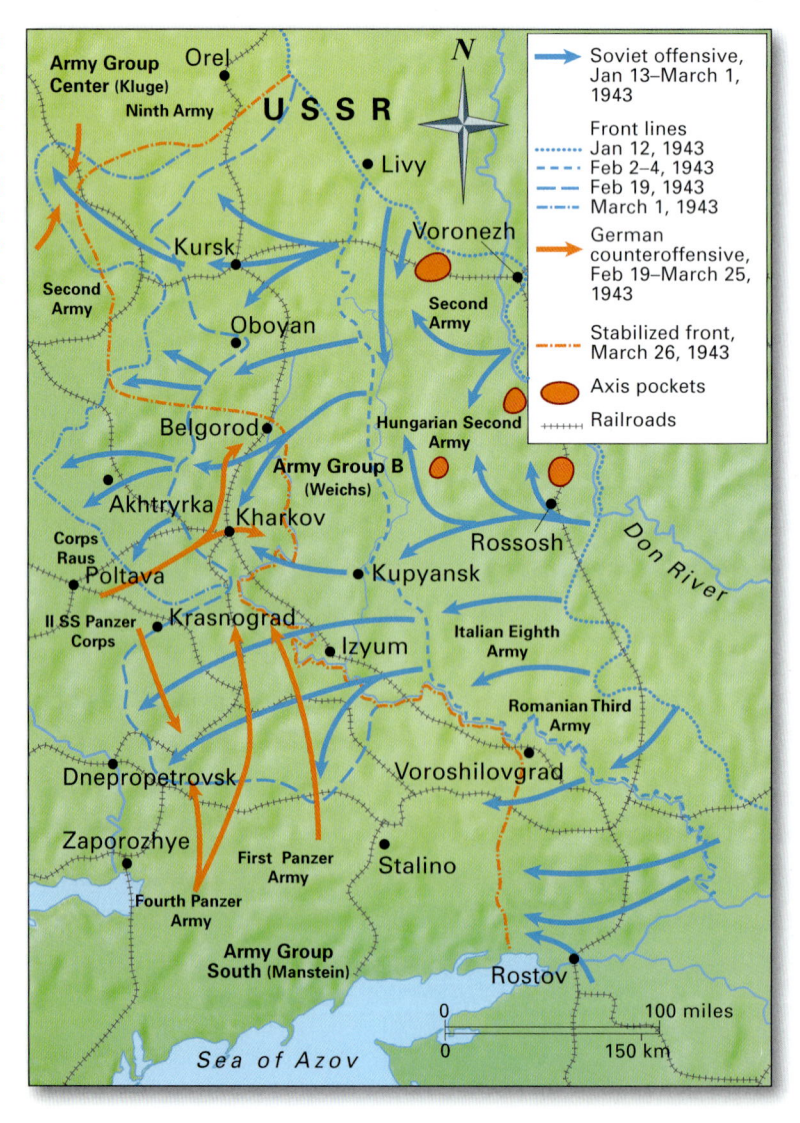

76 THE TIDE TURNS IN EASTERN EUROPE

WAFFEN SS

STRATEGY & TACTICS

The soldiers of the Waffen SS were supposed to be the embodiment of Nazism. But their battlefield prowess was marred by atrocities against civilians and enemy personnel. The Waffen SS (Combat SS) was part of the much larger SS or *Schutzstaffel* (Defense Unit), run by Heinrich Himmler. The Waffen SS was formed in 1939. Initially, it was a small organization, but it expanded to thirty-nine divisions. At first, its members had to be dedicated Nazis, of "pure" German blood, and swear allegiance to Adolf Hitler. By the end of the war, it included about 900,000 men of non-German origin.

On the eastern front the Waffen SS led many attacks or was used as a "fire brigade," rushing between threatened sectors to prevent a Red Army breakthrough. As fighting broke out on other fronts, Waffen SS units fought in Italy, the Balkans, and western Europe. Their excellent fighting reputation was only partly deserved. The quality of the Waffen SS soldier in general was hurt by numerous atrocities against both civilians and Allied soldiers. Scores of Waffen SS members were tried and convicted of war crimes after the war.

Kursk: Germany's Last Eastern Offensive

Even as Manstein was succeeding at Kharkov, the German army's chief of staff wanted to erase the recently created Kursk salient, or bulge, in the central region of the eastern front. Field Marshal Gunther von Kluge, commanding Army Group Center, was on the northern sector of the bulge. Field Marshal von Manstein's Kharkov victory had his Army Group South on the southern shoulder of the bulge. Drives from north and south might trap or destroy the Russian forces around Kursk. This plan could delay, if not prevent, the Red Army's expected offensive. The proposed maneuver, code-named Operation Citadel, had merits. It did not take into account the growing confidence and skill of the Red Army and its commanders.

The German high command was divided over the need for the offensive. Hitler agreed to Operation Citadel in mid-April but General Heinz Guderian, Inspector-General of Armored Troops, argued that the attack would lead to heavy tank losses. He wanted to move armored forces to western Europe, as a reserve against the Allied invasion expected some time in 1944. Hitler overruled all his generals and set July 5 for Operation Citadel.

THE TIDE TURNS IN EASTERN EUROPE, 1942 TO 1943

Operation Citadel relied on an element of surprise. But a network of Soviet spies warned the Red Army of the plan. As the start date of the offensive neared, Soviet reinforcements flooded into the bulge. Extensive lines of defenses, covered by mines, barbed wire, and antitank guns, were built. On the eve of battle two Soviet army groups manned lines that varied in depth between 15 and 25 miles (24 and 40 km). Two million German and Soviet troops and 6,000 tanks were ready for battle.

On July 5 Operation Citadel opened with a Russian bombardment of the Ninth Army. Seven German armored divisions gained only 5 miles (8 km) on the first day and recorded severe losses of both tanks and men. After a week of similar fighting, the Ninth Army had only moved 12 miles (20 km). Its attacks had run out of steam. Matters were initially better on the southern sector of the bulge. That attack was led by the 4th Panzer Army and Operational Group Kampf of General von Manstein's Army Group South.

The panzer army received substantial reinforcements, most notably from elite Waffen SS divisions and advanced 20 miles (32 km) by July 11. Yet the two arms of the German pincer attack were still 75 miles (120 km) apart. The German attacks effectively ended on July 12, when the counterattacking Russian 5th Guards Tank Army fought General Hermann Hoth's 4th Panzer Army to a standstill around the village of Prokhorovka.

A day later Hitler met von Manstein and Kluge at Rastenburg, his secret headquarters in East Prussia. General von Manstein argued that Kluge had to hold up the bulk of the Soviet forces in the bulge. Kluge felt too weak to do so. Hitler intervened and ordered the end of Operation Citadel.

Russia's Summer Offensives

The failure of Citadel confirmed that Germany had lost the initiative on the eastern front. Outnumbered and outgunned by the Red Army, it could only fight defensively. In the longer term it suffered due to a near-constant stream of casualties and the steady transfer of units to counter Allied threats in Italy and western Europe. In contrast the Red Army was growing ever larger, better equipped, and confident of victory. The Soviets were able to launch a succession of major offensives all along the eastern front during the remainder of the year.

By August 15 the German defense had been penetrated at several points. The strain of defending a long front line with limited resources was beginning to show. Russian partisan groups made matters worse. The groups had been ordered to destroy railroads behind the German lines to halt the flow of reinforcements and supplies eastward. General von Manstein, defending a 650-mile (1,040-km) front stretching from the Kursk bulge to the Sea of Azov, was also under pressure from several Soviet army groups. By early August the German general was arguing that he had to retreat or suffer severe losses, even though a retreat might lead to the loss of sources of coal, manganese, and iron ore.

General von Manstein was not alone in contemplating withdrawal to save his troops, and reduce the length of supply lines. Many other generals agreed with his position. Hitler stubbornly refused to contemplate surrendering any territory in the east.

> *Hitler stubbornly refused to contemplate surrendering any territory in the east.*

Hitler ordered General von Manstein to hold Kharkov at all costs, but the field marshal faced a major Soviet counterattack. In defiance of his orders, he abandoned Kharkov on August 23. He undertook a skillfully conducted retreat. His troops destroyed everything of value as they fell back. The Red Army kept up the pressure through September and October. Manstein's troops retreated through the Ukraine, abandoning Kiev to General Nikolai Vatutin's 1st Ukrainian Front on the night of November 5–6. The Red Army forces established bridgeheads on the west bank of the Dnieper River.

By the end of 1943, the Soviet pressure on Germany was relentless. The Germans surrendered huge swaths of territory and suffered immense losses. Only the Leningrad area appeared stable, but the Red Army was poised to break the siege during January 1944. The offensive was a prelude to further attacks all along the line to liberate the western Soviet Union. Once again the German army would have to fight for its life. The long retreats of 1943 were a sign of further disasters for Nazi Germany.

▶ Members of the Dutch resistance overcome the German camera ban by taking pictures with a hidden camera.

6 Occupation, Resistance, and Collaboration

KEY PLACES		
Western Europe	Eastern Europe	Asia

At the height of its power, Nazi Germany occupied a large amount of territory. European countries under German control in early 1942 included France, Belgium, the Netherlands, Poland, Luxembourg, Denmark, Norway, Finland, Estonia, Latvia, Lithuania, parts of Russia, Ukraine, Yugoslavia, and also Greece, as well as Morocco, Algeria, and Tunisia in North Africa. After the fall of Mussolini in July 1943, Germany also occupied the northern half of Italy.

In Asia, Japan had made similar conquests. Following the attack on Pearl Harbor in December 1941, Malaya (now Malaysia), Hong Kong, the Philippines, the Dutch East Indies (now Indonesia), Singapore, French Indochina, and Burma fell. This gave Japan dominance in the Pacific.

As a result of these conquests, millions of people around the world had to adjust to life under Axis occupation.

Administering German Occupation

The Greater German Reich, Hitler's empire, was dominated from Berlin. All forms of self-expression and self-determination were tightly controlled or crushed. An occupied country was governed in one of three ways: directly by the Third Reich, under a civil administration based on German policies and laws, or by military force. Western Europe generally fell into the first two categories. Most of occupied southern and eastern Europe endured military government.

At the end of 1942, the Nazi empire in Europe expanded into occupied countries and extended its influence into Axis satellites. A few countries remained neutral.

Life under German Occupation

In the occupied territories, Nazi rule influenced all aspects of daily life. Each individual was issued new identity papers. Failure to produce these papers when asked could result in serious penalties, including imprisonment or execution. Curfews were imposed at night. Anyone found on the streets after curfew could be arrested or shot on the spot.

Standards of living plummeted. The Germans took the best food and goods available. In France people made coffee out of acorns because regular coffee went to the Germans. Gasoline was almost impossible for civilians to get. German businessmen could buy goods at very low prices. The Germans imposed "occupation costs" and took them directly out of government finances. Denmark provided agricultural produce to feed more than 8 million Germans, while the Danes themselves nearly starved.

The occupied territories provided the Germans with vast amounts of forced labor. In 1939, for example, 301,000 foreign civilians were transported to the Reich as workers. They made up 0.8 percent of the workforce in the German economy. By 1944 this figure had risen to 5,295,000 foreign civilians. Combined with 1,831,000 prisoner-of-war laborers, foreign workers made up 24 percent of the German workforce. Belgium provided more than 95,000 workers for the metal industry and Poland gave nearly 1.5 million laborers.

In the occupied territories, Nazi rule influenced all aspects of daily life.

To house the huge influx of forced labor, more than 20,000 work camps sprang up around Germany. Conditions varied greatly. Generally, the laborers employed in factories received the best treatment and food. Those in mining, agriculture, and construction were treated worse. Jewish or Soviet peoples were forced to live in subhuman conditions no matter what their employment. A typical daily menu might consist of two bowls of thin vegetable soup for breakfast and lunch, and a single hunk of bread in the evening. Once a week the workers might receive a small piece of meat. Combined with long hours of work, these living conditions resulted in chronic sickness and fatalities among workers.

The German Gestapo

The main source of terror in the occupied territories was the Gestapo, the political police section of the German Reich Security Main Office. The Gestapo had 30,000 agents that scoured Germany and the occupied territories for people who committed crimes against the Nazi Party or the German state. Torture and threat were the methods of investigation. The Gestapo could issue an "order for protective custody," which meant they could imprison anyone indefinitely without trial. Most people who were taken into "protective custody" simply disappeared. They were murdered in one of the many Gestapo headquarters across Europe.

Most people who were taken into "protective custody" simply disappeared.

Eastern Europe suffered more than any other region during the occupation. In Nazi eyes, Poles, Baltic Europeans, and Russians did not have human rights. In Poland and occupied Russian territories, SS death squads known as *Einsatzgruppen* slaughtered anyone they thought was a threat. They targeted Jews and intellectuals, but thousands of other civilians also suffered. More than 531 Polish towns and villages were burned to the ground in 1939 alone. Every aspect of Polish cultural life was destroyed, including libraries, theaters, museums, street signs, and books. Worst of all, almost the entire Polish Jewish population—2.5 million people—were executed or worked to death in extermination and labor camps.

Eastern Europe suffered more than any other region during the occupation.

The occupied Russian territories fared no better. The Einsatzgruppen massacred 1.5 million Jewish civilians there, and a similar number of other citizens. In late September of 1941, in the ravine of Babi Yar near Kiev, Ukraine, SS soldiers shot dead 33,771 Russian Jews in one forty-eight-hour period. It was not only the SS that committed atrocities. The German army would deliberately burn or occupy entire villages. People were left to starve or freeze to death. Almost all agriculture was controlled by the Germans, who left little for the Russian people.

PEOPLE AND WAR

GERMAN REPRISALS

Reprisal was the main tool used by the Germans to crush resistance. Whenever German soldiers were killed or military property damaged, Wehrmacht or SS units would exact revenge to prevent further resistance. One of the most infamous reprisals occurred at Oradour-sur-Glane in France on June 10, 1944. Resistance was active in the area, so a company of the 2nd SS Panzer Division were sent to Oradour. All the villagers were gathered in the town square. The women and children were placed in a church, and the men put among five barns. SS soldiers set all the buildings on fire, thereby burning most of the occupants to death. They machine-gunned those who tried to escape. In all, 642 French civilians were murdered.

The assassination of SS leader Reinhard Heydrich by resistance fighters in Czechoslovakia led to reprisals in which about 1,000 people were shot. In the village of Lidice in June 1942, all 198 men were shot and the women and children sent to concentration camps. Every building was obliterated, and the ground levelled. Crops were planted over the site. The village's name was removed from German maps. In Russia, a single German soldier's death at the hands of partisans could lead to an entire village being razed and its occupants massacred. Reprisals reduced the level of resistance and increased collaboration between the villagers and the enemy. To protect themselves, local people were prepared to betray their own village's resistance fighters.

The Japanese Occupation

In many ways the Japanese occupation of their new empire was just as harsh as Germany's. The Japanese, however, had a different agenda. In July 1940 the Japanese government formally proclaimed the Greater East Asia Co-Prosperity Sphere. This policy aimed at expelling colonial powers from Asia. In its place the Japanese proclaimed a new order based on national self-rule, with Asia free from colonizers. Japan promoted itself as the liberator of Asia.

The character of Japanese rule varied according to place and people. The Dutch East Indies, Hong Kong, Singapore, Borneo, Timor, and New Guinea were all placed under Japanese military government. No self-determination was permitted for the local populations. Malaya was also under military rule, but Japan promised self-rule at a later date. Manchuria (renamed Munchukuo by the Japanese) and occupied China were ruled and exploited by a Japanese administration. Indochina—consisting of Vietnam, Laos, and Cambodia—was a colony of Vichy France. Despite being occupied by Japanese forces, it was administered by the Vichy French government until 1945. Burma was also allowed a civil administration.

> *Such operations became known as the "three alls"— kill all, burn all, loot all.*

Japanese rule was severe, particularly for Europeans, U.S. citizens, and Allied prisoners of war (POWs). In Singapore European families were interned in prison camps. Men were often sent to work constructing the Thailand–Burma railroad, known as the Death Railway. They were joined by 61,000 Australian, British, and Dutch POWs and 270,000 civilians from Burma, Thailand, Malaya, and the Dutch East Indies. Ill-fed, beaten, ravaged by disease, and worked to the point of collapse, thousands of workers died. To cut the railroad through 240 miles (386 km) of dense jungle cost over 100,000 lives, nearly 500 people for every mile of track laid.

Conditions in Japanese prison camps were almost as bad. Thousands of European prisoners died of disease and malnutrition. People of mixed Asian and European descent could be executed because their parents had "collaborated" with the enemy. Local people had to bow to any Japanese soldier they passed. In a region where the bow is a sign of respect, this was humiliating. Anyone not bowing would be beaten or killed. In China, Japanese troops might descend on a village, slaughtering every inhabitant and looting everything of value. Such operations became known as the "three alls"—kill all, burn all, loot all.

The occupied territories were important to Japan's war effort. Japan was almost entirely dependent on other countries for raw metals, rubber, oil, and food. In 1940 alone, Japan imported 7 billion tons of coal, 2.3 billion tons of iron ore, 22 million barrels of oil, and 445,000 tons of rice from the occupied territories. Governments from most occupied territories proclaimed their support for Japan. But occupation did not have the backing of common people. Poor and starving, they were experiencing Japanese cruelty first-hand. The Japanese ruled by force, not popularity.

Collaboration with the Enemy

Collaboration, or working with the enemy, existed in many forms. Poland, for example, was occupied for nearly five years. Most citizens interacted with the Germans on some level, from serving them in a store to providing them with transport. In Belgium collaboration of this kind was common. After the war 53,000 people were convicted of *la politique du moindre mal*, meaning the "policy of doing the least harm."

Collaboration could also be profitable. By the fall of 1942, French businessmen had made deals with their German masters worth 4 billion reichsmarks. In the aircraft industry, France produced 3,620 aircraft and 11,783 airplane engines for the German war machine. Furthermore, many people wanted to work for the Germans to maintain their wealth. More than 400,000 Belgians willingly found work in Germany, part of 2 million voluntary workers in the German Reich by August 1941.

POLITICAL WORLD: VIDKUN QUISLING: NORWEGIAN COLLABORATION

In World War II, Vidkun Quisling's name became synonymous with collaboration. Anyone labeled a Quisling was deemed a traitor to his or her country. Quisling (1887–1945) was the founder of a Norwegian Fascist organization called the Fascist National Union Party (FNUP). Created during the 1930s, the FNUP received funding from the German Nazi Party in the late 1930s. Once the German campaign in Europe began, Quisling met with Adolf Hitler and offered to overthrow the Norwegian government. Quisling wanted to establish a Fascist government with himself in charge and to use everything at his disposal for the German war effort. Hitler turned down his offer of help and occupied Norway in April 1940.

Quisling exploited his links with the Germans. In February 1942 he was proclaimed minister-president of Norway. His new position was weak, despite its title. The Norwegian people rigorously opposed his attempts to make Norway a Nazi state. Quisling remained a dangerous man, however. After a single Norwegian policeman offended him in 1943, he had 470 policeman sent in retaliation to German concentration camps. Up to 1,000 Jews suffered a similar fate as Quisling attempted to impress his German masters.

Quisling's fate was sealed when Norway was liberated by the Allies in May 1945. He was captured and tried for treason and other crimes. Once found guilty, he was executed.

Even in eastern Europe, where German persecution was at its worst, collaboration was common. Ukraine suffered under Stalin prior to the war. Many Ukrainians saw the Germans almost as liberators. Up to 1.2 million Ukrainian volunteers, known as Hiwis from the German for "volunteer auxiliaries," worked as laborers for the Germans. Even in Poland, nearly 250,000 workers went voluntarily to Germany in 1940 alone to escape unemployment at home.

At the other end of the scale was outright collaboration, that is, actively assisting the Germans in their war effort. The most famous collaborators were part of the Vichy regime in France. The Vichy government was a pro-German civil administration established after France fell to the Germans on June 22, 1940. The government was created at Vichy in southeastern France on July 10, 1940. Marshal Philippe Pétain was its head. He was assisted by Pierre Laval, an ambitious politician.

Technically, the Vichy government controlled both the occupied and unoccupied parts of France. Yet the German authorities in Paris closely monitored Vichy leadership and decisions. It changed the slogan of the French republic from "Liberty, Equality, Fraternity" to the more Germanic "Work, Family, Fatherland." The Vichy authorities also helped deport French Jewish citizens from the camps in southern France to extermination camps. Laval even broadcast a message on June 22, 1942, stating the the Vichy regime backed the German victory over the Soviet Union. Some Vichy French troops actually fought Allied units in North Africa in November 1942. Most did not, however, and Vichy authority crumbled. On November 11, Germany took over the unoccupied zone of France and almost all of its government. The Vichy regime's power effectively ended. Its administration remains one of the most controversial periods in French history.

At the other end of the scale was outright collaboration— actively assisting the Germans in their war effort.

In Norway Vidkun Quisling, a Fascist politician, embraced Nazi ideology. Though he was made Norwegian minister-president on February 1, 1942, his officials were little more than figureheads for German power.

EYEWITNESS

SIMHA ROTEM

Simha Rotem was a resistance fighter during the Warsaw uprising in occupied Poland in 1943. In this extract he describes the terrible event.

> German shouts rang out, ordering the inhabitants to leave their apartments and report to the courtyard. We consulted on the spot and decided to stay inside. The Germans repeated the announcement twice more, warning that the house would be destroyed along with all the occupants. Nevertheless, we didn't move. We heard band music played by German soldiers in the yard: was that the signal to start the operation? This is one of my strangest memories: everything around going up in flames, walls caving in—and that music. Through the window I saw the players blowing into their instruments, and I stood still, hypnotized. Walls were collapsing, people were being killed, and there they stood and played... A few seconds later, the building was set on fire by flamethrowers and went up in a blaze. Smoke penetrated the apartment and it was hard to breathe.
>
> We ran to a lower floor and entered an apartment that had been broken open. What with the rising smoke and the commotion, I lost part of the group. Irena, Marysia, and Stefan stayed with me. The others—Yosef Sak, Stasia, and Krysia—disappeared. ...The whole time the Germans stood in the courtyard and continued to play.

Extract taken from Simha Rotem (Kazik), *Memoirs of a Warsaw Ghetto Fighter: The Past Within Me* (London and New Haven, Yale University Press, 1994).

Greece formed a pro-German administration headed by General Georgios Tsolakoglou. Croatia, a region of Yugoslavia, declared itself an independent pro-German state under Ante Paveliæ. Croatia declared war on the Allies and killed Jewish and Serbian people within its territories. In the Netherlands the Dutch Nazi Party under Anton Mussert had 50,000 members, of whom 17,000 went into service with the German Waffen SS.

In the Far East, Asian governments supported the Japanese. Thailand, for example, received territory from Malaya and Burma in return for helping Japan. Burma itself had pro-Japanese governments, including the violent Burma Independence Army. Yet collaboration in East Asia never really took root. The Japanese treated the peoples they conquered with hatred and contempt. As a result, resistance and defiance became prevalent.

In the West probably the most extreme form of collaboration was to join the German armed forces. Most who joined in western Europe were members of Fascist organizations before the occupation. The Netherlands had an active Fascist party, and produced many recruits for German military service. In eastern Europe, civilians joined to fight against the Soviet regime, which had persecuted many ethnic groups before the war.

Only the most ideologically extreme individuals were willing to fight against the Allies.

Only the most ideologically extreme individuals were willing to fight against the Allies. Most ended up in the Waffen SS, the political combat units of the Nazi Party responsible for some of the worst actions of World War II. Foreign volunteers were formed into special divisions. Between 1944 and 1945 Norway, Holland, Denmark, Latvia, Croatia, Ukraine, Hungary, Estonia, Albania, Italy, Belgium, Belarus, and Russia produced enough volunteers to form twenty-one divisions of Waffen SS soldiers. Most of them served either on the Russian front or in the war against the partisans in Yugoslavia.

Resistance in Europe

Throughout occupied Europe resistance groups published underground newspapers and pamphlets that attacked the German system. Resistance literature was printed on illegal printing presses deep underground in cellars and distributed by brave individuals. One French resistance paper had a circulation of 400,000. Anyone caught working with a paper would be arrested and usually executed or deported to a concentration camp.

Much resistance activity was supported by secret service organizations in Britain and the United States. In 1941, an unusual campaign began in Belgium—the "V" campaign. British prime minister Winston Churchill had made the V "for victory" hand signal a symbol of resistance in Britain. In Belgium, the V also stood for freedom. Soon its citizens were putting the V symbol on houses, walls, and even German military buildings and vehicles as a sign of their resistance. The phenomenon spread throughout occupied Europe and helped people unite against the Germans.

Spying was perhaps the most important form of resistance. Civilians would observe or photograph German military units, documents, and positions. The information was then sent to Allied intelligence agencies. The agencies provided equipment for use in these spying operations. This equipment included miniature cameras for photographing documents and high-powered radios and encoding systems for broadcasting back to British listening stations. It was very dangerous work. Most spies who were caught were tortured by the Gestapo and eventually executed.

Prior to the invasion of occupied France on June 6, 1944, French resistance operators mapped the German defenses along the Atlantic coast. Maps were smuggled to Britain aboard fishing vessels at great personal risk. Some resistance groups wanted a more aggressive approach. They blew up German trains and railroads, launched ambushes against vehicle columns, and killed German sentries. In 1942 a number of French citizens fled to the forests and mountains to escape from forced labor deportation. The resistance group they formed became known as the Maquis, meaning "scrub" or "jungle." They lived off the land. Over the next two years they bombed and assassinated with weapons supplied by airdrops from Britain.

Spying was perhaps the most important form of resistance.

The activities of the Maquis increased before the Allied invasion in June 1944. Hundreds of miles of railroads were destroyed in an attempt to damage the German supply routes. After the invasion, thousands of civilians took up arms in Paris, trying to liberate the capital themselves. The cost to the country of the invasion resistance was high. About 100,000 people were executed or deported by the Germans.

Other western European countries had resistance movements. For example, Norway recruited up to 40,000 operators. Perhaps its most significant resistance achievement was the destruction of the Norsk Hydrogen Electrolysis plant in Vermork, Telemark. The plant was vital to Germany's planned development of atomic weapons. On February 28, 1943, British-trained Norwegian resistance fighters broke into the plant and destroyed it with explosives, thereby removing the German atomic threat.

Resistance in western Europe generally did not approach the scale of that in eastern Europe and Yugoslavia. Poland had possibly the most potent resistance movement of all. Between 1941 and 1944, groups such as the Polish Home Army, the People's Guard, and the Jewish Fighting Organization derailed 803 railway locomotives, destroyed more than 4,000 German vehicles, burned fifteen German factories to the ground, and blew up thirty-eight railway bridges. This activity led to two uprisings against German occupation in Warsaw, the Polish capital. The first occurred on April 19, 1943. Around 1,000 Jews fought for three weeks against SS soldiers attempting to round up Jews for deportation to concentration camps. Eventually the uprising was crushed. Almost all the resistance fighters were killed either in the battle itself or executed.

The second uprising occurred on August 1, 1944, and suffered a similar fate. The Polish Home Army attempted to seize power before the Russians advanced from the east and took over the city. Just under 38,000 Polish resistance fighters battled for two months, capturing sections of the city and killing around 17,000 German soldiers. Using units from the SS and all available air and artillery power, the furious Germans destroyed 80 percent of Warsaw. Around 250,000 Polish citizens were slaughtered. Polish resistance effectively ended.

In occupied Russia, partisan warfare was the main way of resistance. The partisans were made up of Red Army soldiers trapped behind enemy lines during the German advance. As the partisan force grew in size, agents of the NKVD, the Soviet secret service, attempted to organize guerrilla-style resistance. The partisans recruited through a mixture of terror and force and by mid-1943 they numbered around 250,000. Against them were 500,000 German troops dedicated to antipartisan activities. Reprisals for partisan attacks were dreadful. Hundreds of Russian men, women, and children could be slaughtered in response to the killing of a single German soldier. But Stalin kept pressure on the partisans to continue their work.

In southern Europe, Yugoslavia was the center of a partisan war that cost 1.4 million lives. Huge numbers of Yugoslavian army soldiers disap-

> *Almost all resistance fighters were killed either in the battle itself or executed.*

OSS AND SOE

STRATEGY & TACTICS

The Office of Strategic Services (OSS) and the Special Operations Executive (SOE) were the main U.S. and British organizations for promoting resistance in and gathering intelligence from the occupied territories. The OSS was created on June 13, 1942. OSS intelligence activities fell under several branches. The Special Operations Branch conducted missions in enemy territory, including sabotage, spying, and psychological missions such as dropping propaganda leaflets. The Research and Analysis branch was more scholarly. It relied on experts to produce detailed information about the countries in which the agents would operate. A technical department produced equipment required for the missions.

The OSS conducted missions across all Allied theaters. Operations included gathering intelligence for the Operation Torch landings in North Africa in late 1942, training and fighting with Yugoslavian partisans, training Austrian and German refugees for spying duties inside Germany itself, and gathering intelligence against the Japanese from bases in China and Burma. Once the war ended, the OSS was shut down by President Truman on September 20, 1945.

The SOE had a narrower focus than the OSS. It used espionage, sabotage, and propaganda to destabilize Axis forces. Established in July 1940, the SOE brought together departments from British secret-service organizations. The SOE recruited thousands of civilian and military personnel as agents for high-risk foreign missions. Most recruits were highly educated. They had to be quick-thinking, intelligent, and independent.

Trained SOE agents were usually dropped into enemy-occupied countries. They were expected to blend into the population and spy on the enemy. In Europe and Asia, the SOE promoted, trained, and equipped resistance movements.

Resistance fighters could use courier and escape routes to pass along information in occupied Europe (1940–1945).

OCCUPATION, RESISTANCE, AND COLLABORATION

peared into the country's inaccessible mountains after the German occupation. From there they launched a guerrilla war against both the Germans and each other. The Yugoslavian resistance was split between the Chetniks, forces loyal to Colonel Draza Mihajlovic, and those who followed the Communist partisan leader Josip Broz, known as Tito. At first the two groups cooperated, but relations between them soon broke down over the civilian cost of reprisals. A civil war erupted. Chetniks began cooperated with the German and Italian occupiers. Tito resisted the Axis powers and received strong support from Britain, through the OSS and SOE.

In Italy, after the downfall of the dictator Mussolini in July 1943, German forces occupied the northern half of the country. Bands of Italian partisans operated in the mountainous Alpine and Apennine regions. Most partisans were former soldiers who wanted the Nazis to leave Italy. Others were civilians motivated by Communist politics. By late 1944 this "Voluntary Freedom Corps" numbered more than 100,000. They raided German positions in northern Italy and suffered huge losses in an all-out German offensive against the partisans in September 1944. More than 40,000 Italian partisans died in the war, but they also made life difficult for German forces defending northern Italy.

In Italy, after the downfall of the dictator Mussolini in July 1943, German forces occupied the northern half of the country.

Resistance in East Asia

Resistance against Japanese occupation did not reach the same scale as in Europe. Partly this was due to effective Japanese rule, and partly to the difficulty of supplying resistance movements in areas of dense jungle.

Much resistance was passive. In the Philippines, for example, when the Japanese imposed the Japanese language and curriculum on Filipino schools, most of the locals responded by simply keeping their children away from school altogether. Yet armed resistance was also present. The Philippines had large areas uninhabited by the Japanese, which were ideal for resistance groups. The main group was the *Hukbalahap*, or People's

Anti-Japanese Army (PAJA). The PAJA partisans were masters of the jungle. They also assassinated wealthy Filipinos for collaboration. By 1945 they were strong enough to establish their own government in the area around Luzon.

A key value of resistance groups was to give information to the Allies about Japanese movements in East Asia. Both British and U.S. intelligence supported Asian resistance. In Thailand the Free Thai resistance movement was sponsored by the OSS (the Office of Strategic Services) to cross into Thailand from Allied-occupied China and spy on Japanese units. More than 10,000 OSS-trained resistance fighters also operated in Burma and assisted the British with major maneuvers. Communist guerrillas in Indochina also spied for the OSS.

The British were heavily involved in training guerrilla movements. Resistance fighters in Singapore, Burma, and Malaya were taught combat skills by teams from SOE. Malaya produced a successful resistance unit, the Malayan People's Anti-Japanese Army. It consisted of Chinese and Malayan guerrillas who made small-scale strikes against Japanese units. The guerrillas numbered around 7,000 by the end of war, and killed 2,600 enemy soldiers or officials.

The military effect of resistance movements on the Japanese was small. Worldwide, resistance contributed more to the morale of occupied peoples than to the downfall of the Axis. However, resistance to occupation seems to be natural for those who value the freedom of their own countries.

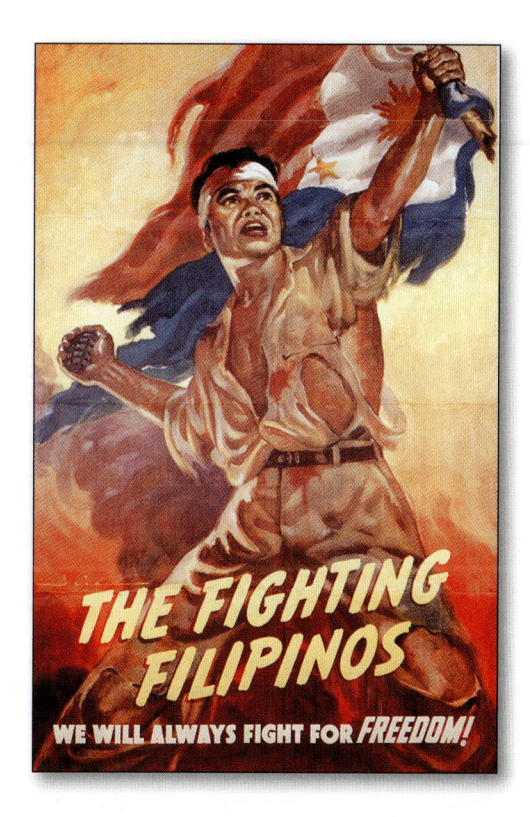

A propaganda poster for the Filipino resistance movement against the Japanese.

OCCUPATION, RESISTANCE, AND COLLABORATION 95

▶ Now a museum piece, this American-made light tank was used successfully by the British in North Africa.

7 North Africa, 1942 to 1943

KEY PEOPLE	KEY PLACES
Field Marshal Erwin Rommel	Cyrenaica, Libya
General Claude Auchinleck	El Alamein, Egypt
General Bernard Montgomery	Tunis, Tunisia
Major General George S. Patton	Tobruk, Libya

The situation for Axis forces in North Africa in January 1942 looked bleak. The Allied Eighth Army under General Claude Auchinleck, commander in chief of the Middle East Command, had driven Rommel's Panzer Group Africa back over across Libya for 600 miles (965 km). Territory that had been brilliantly snatched by Field Marshal Erwin Rommel, between March and May 1941 was reclaimed. Losses totaled 38,000 men, 340 tanks, and 300 aircraft. The Allies saw victory at hand.

They had not, however, taken into account Rommel's genius. They had also not noticed improvements in the German tactical position. Heavy air bombardment of the Allied island of Malta eased movement for German shipping in the Mediterranean. In the early weeks of 1942 German convoys reached Tripoli, the Libyan capital, increasing Rommel's tanks to more than one hundred machines. Ammunition, fuel, and troops were restocked. On paper the Allies were still stronger, but the Germans had superiority in combined air, armor, antitank, and infantry operations.

Rommel's New Offensive

General Auchinleck planned a resumed push for Tripoli. On January 21, 1942, Rommel boldly counterattacked with the full force of his Panzer Army Africa. The starting point was El Agheila on the Libyan coast to the west. The German Afrika Korps troops, along with the Italian X, XI, and XII Corps, advanced steadily along the coastline of Cyrenaica, a territory in northern Libya. The next day they reached and took Agedabia, 100 miles (160 km) to the east. Then the Axis forces drove into the interior of Cyrenaica. Msus was captured on January 25. There, Rommel's forces split. The Italians cut to the coastal city of Benghazi. The German forces attacked from Msus toward the northern and eastern coast. The Allies evacuated Benghazi to escape encirclement. Rommel's forces captured vital Allied airfields and later used them for bombing raids on Malta.

The Allies collapsed under an attack that used antitank guns, tanks, and infantry.

The Allies collapsed under an attack that used antitank guns, tanks, and infantry. German tanks gave covering fire while the guns were moved into position, and vice versa. This meant that Allied armor faced constant gunfire. German infantry, meanwhile, dealt with enemy artillery positions. British armor was wasted because of poor tactics. British tanks went into action as separate units rather than in full force. This tactic enabled the Germans to destroy these forces as they appeared, even though the Allies had more tanks.

By February 5 and 6, Rommel had advanced over 400 miles (644 km). He settled into defensive positions in the town of Tmimi on the northeastern coast of Cyrenaica. The Allies were about 50 miles (80 km) away, in defensive positions known as the Gazala Line.

Gazala and Beyond

The Gazala Line stretched about 50 miles (80 km) south from just west of Gazala to Bir Hakeim. It had deep minefields, and behind them groups from XIII Corps set up defensive pockets. The focus of XXX Corps was to protect against German attempts to outflank from the south. In theory, soldiers along the Gazala Line would break apart any frontal attack.

In practice, the British defenses failed. The Gazala Line positions were too widely spaced to form strong fields of fire. The British did have more tanks—850 plus 420 tanks in reserve against an Axis force of 560 vehicles. The British also had greater superiority in terms of artillery. But numbers alone could not guarantee supremacy.

Auchinleck made preparations for a June offensive. Once again Rommel performed a pre-emptive action. On the afternoon of May 26, the Italian X and XI Corps attacked the northern half of the Gazala Line. At 9:00 p.m. Rommel sent the German 15th and 21st Panzer Divisions, the 90th Infantry Division, and the Italian XX Corps on a flanking attack southward.

The attack aimed to drive around the bottom of the Gazala Line at Bir Hakeim, cut up the coast, capture the port of Tobruk, and surround the forces on the Gazala Line. Rommel's assault did not go according to plan. Allied units in the south responded to the German drive with newly supplied American Grant tanks. These had high-velocity 75-mm (2.9-in.) guns with a longer range than the 50-mm (1.9-in.) weapons of the Panzer IIIs.

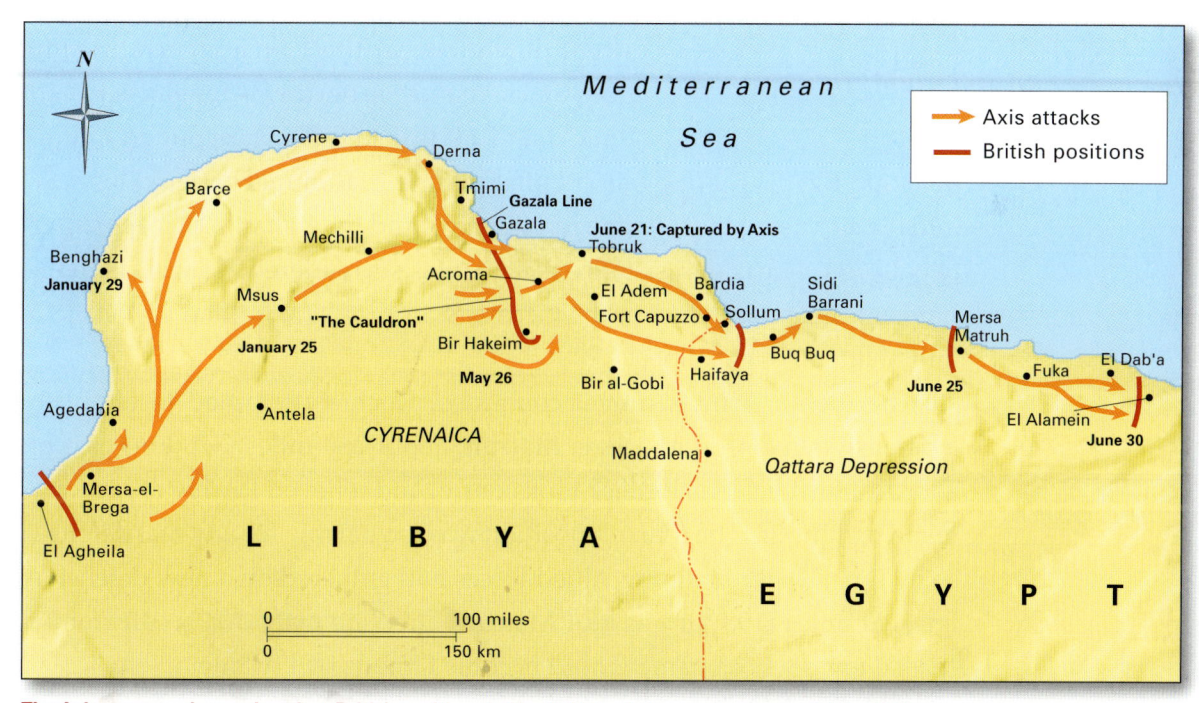

The Axis powers advanced against British positions in North Africa between January and July 1942.

NORTH AFRICA, 1942 TO 1943 99

Rommel realized that the northern coast objective was no longer viable. Fuel, food, and water were low. Over 30 percent of German armor was destroyed by June 1. He redirected his lead units to assault 150 Brigade in the center of the Gazala Line. The area of battle, an oval-shaped area 10 miles (16 km) long and 7 miles (11 km) wide, became known as the Cauldron. Allied and Axis armor and infantry fought fiercely. On May 31 and June 1, 150 Brigade was effectively destroyed. British planes flew constant ground-attack missions, depleting Rommel's damaged forces.

The German troops in the Cauldron constructed good defensive positions and antitank barriers. The British Eighth Army commander, Major General Neil Ritchie, repeated past mistakes. Ineffective British armor was hammered by accurate antitank and panzer fire. By June 6, 230 Allied fighting vehicles had been lost. More than 4,000 Allied soldiers were captured, and four regiments of artillery destroyed. Rommel sensed that the Allies' will to fight was collapsing. On June 11 Rommel's troops made a southern breakout from the Cauldron. They swept down to clear the 1 Free French Brigade from Bir Hakeim, then northward again. Between June 11 and 14, British units were put on full retreat into Egypt. Tobruk was cut off. On June 20 Rommel battered his way into the city using his two panzer divisions and the Italian XX Corps. After twenty-four hours of resistance the city was surrendered. As well as thousands of men and vehicles, the Germans acquired 2.2 million gallons (8.3 million liters) of gasoline.

The Eighth Army's retreat continued. Ritchie attempted to establish a defensive line around Mersa Matruh, about 230 miles (370 km) east of Tobruk. However, Auchinleck took control and relieved Ritchie of his command on June 25. The Matruh position was too narrow for any real defense, so by June 30 all remaining Allied forces had gathered on a new defensive line 120 miles (193 km) east of Matruh. This line extended south from a coastal town whose name would become famous—El Alamein.

El Alamein

Three successive battles at El Alamein marked the turning point in North Africa. Although it did not have the obvious defensive positions of Mersa Matruh or the Gazala Line, El Alamein had geographical advantages. At the southern end of the line, only 30 miles (48 km) from the Mediterranean coast, lay the Qattara Depression. This desert region of marshes and quicksands was unusable by armored formations. The Qattara Depression would prevent Rommel from making attacks from the south. The Ruweisat Ridge, running west–east just south of El Alamein, provided some strategic high ground.

> Three successive battles at El Alamein marked the turning point in North Africa.

Most importantly, Rommel's supply lines were stretched to the breaking point. Tobruk lay 250 miles (402 km) to his rear. Only one coast road linked it with El Alamein, and that was under bombardment from Allied fighter-bombers. Victory threatened to undo Rommel's success. Allied losses had been high, but control over the Mediterranean seaways, the possession of Egyptian ports, and U.S. logistical help meant that they could more easily

General Erwin Rommel *(front, standing)* **with the 15th Panzer Division near Tobruk, Libya.**

NORTH AFRICA, 1942 TO 1943

replenish men, equipment, and fuel. The Germans, by contrast, suffered from distant ports, poor supply routes, little fuel, and no air superiority. By July 1 Rommel had 6,400 men, fewer than fifty tanks, and seventy-one guns.

Still, despite his disadvantages, Rommel assaulted El Alamein with great force. The 15th and 21st Panzer Divisions cut across the front line just south of El Alamein on July 1, while the 90th Light Division pushed the 4th Armored Brigade back to El Alamein. Yet the panzer divisions met staunch resistance from the 18th Indian Brigade at Deir al Sheriff. The defense of the Ruweisat Ridge took another two days.

The El Alamein fighting was costly for Rommel. By July 3 he had only twenty-six tanks left, many destroyed by U.S. Sherman tanks. Auchinleck received reinforcements from the 9th Australian Division, which on July 10 and 11 managed to drive the Italian XXI Corps out of Tell el Eisa, 5 miles (8 km) west of El Alamein. The British armored divisions made two counterstrikes against Rommel's troops, one on July 14 and 15, and the other

Italian prisoners captured by the British at El Alamein are led into the area where they will be held.

102 HORRIFIC INVASIONS

on July 21 and 22. Neither was successful, but they inflicted losses on the Germans. On July 22 Rommel called off this first El Alamein offensive. He would have to wait to attack again until he received reinforcements.

After the long retreat across North Africa the Allies were also depleted. Auchinleck decided to settle on the El Alamein line to rebuild. Winston Churchill felt that Auchinleck was being too cautious, so he flew to Cairo to evaluate the situation. Auchinleck resisted pressure from the prime minister for a September offensive. Frustrated by the excessive caution, Churchill replaced Auchinleck with General Harold Alexander as commander in chief Middle East. He also replaced Ritchie with General Bernard Montgomery as commander of the Eighth Army. Even with the change in command, the Allies would not mount a major offensive until late October.

In September Montgomery faced his first major challenge. In August Rommel received an elite German parachute brigade and an Italian division as reinforcements. His tank strength was brought up to 440 although some were outdated. Rommel decided to act before the Allies were ready to strike. On the night of August 30, 1942, the Battle of Alam Halfa began. Rommel launched an offensive across the entire El Alamein front. The 164th Division and Italian Trento and Bologna divisions made diversionary attacks north of the Ruweisat Ridge. In the south, between Bab el Qattara and the Qattara Depression, Rommel pushed forward with four Italian and German divisions. He was aiming for the Alam Halfa Ridge, in the enemy's rear. If this could be overrun, then Rommel's forces would surround the Allies.

> *Winston Churchill felt that Auchinleck was being too cautious, so he flew to Cairo to evaluate the situation.*

From the start the attack was rough. Minefields delayed the advance. Allied planes bombed German columns. Fuel and ammunition ran low. By September 1 only the 15th Panzer Division had managed to reach the Alam Halfa positions. It was soon repelled by Allied armored units. Eventually the Axis units withdrew and established defensive positions.

Knowing that the enemy was weakened, but still fearing Axis defensive power, Montgomery planned for a major offensive at a later date. Resisting pressure from Churchill for a hasty action, Montgomery spent three weeks assembling a force to overwhelm the enemy.

The new Allied Sherman and Grant tanks were equal to the Germans' Mk III and Mk IV panzers.

By October 23, when the third battle of El Alamein began, Rommel had 50,000 troops, 489 tanks, 1,219 artillery pieces, and only 350 working aircraft. The Allies, by contrast, had 104,000 troops, 1,029 tanks, 2,311 artillery pieces, and 530 aircraft. The quality of equipment used by the Allies was also improved. The new Allied Sherman and Grant tanks were equal to the Germans' Mk III and Mk IV panzers. Rommel's stock of 88-mm (3.4-in.) antitank guns was severely depleted. However high the Allied losses were, they could replace them more easily than the Germans could theirs. Moreover, severe illness had forced Rommel to fly home to Germany to be treated.

Operation Lightfoot, as the offensive was known, opened at 9:30 p.m. with an artillery barrage from more than a thousand guns. Thirty minutes later the Allied infantry and armor surged into action. Montgomery's plan was to drive X and XXX Corps hard through the German defenses north of the Miteirya Ridge, 7 miles (11 km) from the coast. Meanwhile, XIII Corps would launch assaults in the far south. The German 15th Panzer Division and the Italian Littorio Division raked the X and XXX Corps with heavy fire. The Allies spent two days clearing narrow channels through deep minefields. Four brigades of Allied tanks penetrated the minefields on October 26. The German antitank guns concentrated their fire.

Montgomery responded with Operation Supercharge. He drew the 7th Armored, 2nd New Zealand, 1st South African, and 4th Indian Divisions north. On October 28 Montgomery made a thrust toward the northern coastline, hoping to take possession of coastal roads. This action faltered in the face of German resistance.

Though none of the Allied assaults went according to plan, the fighting exhausted the Axis defense. The Germans had fewer than fifty tanks; the Allies had more than 600, as well as air superiority. The Afrika Korps had lost 7,000 men. On the evening of November 2 Rommel began to withdraw his units. To cut off the retreating Axis forces, the Allies headed for the northern coast. Each time, the main German forces escaped. The losses were critical, however. El Alamein had cost the Allies 13,560 men dead or wounded. Yet the Germans and Italians suffered 25,000 dead or wounded and 30,000 prisoners, in addition to 1,000 guns and 320 tanks destroyed or captured. With fewer than 8,000 men, twenty-one tanks, and less than one hundred guns, Rommel retreated for more than 1,000 miles (1,600 km) toward Tunisia.

Operation Torch

Throughout 1942 an intense argument raged between British and U.S. commanders and leaders. The Russian leader Joseph Stalin was clamoring for the Allies to begin forceful operations in western Europe. In the United States the chief of staff of the U.S. Army, General George C. Marshall and deputy chief of the War Plans Division, General Dwight D. Eisenhower, argued for an attack into Europe through France. The British prime minister and his advisers, by contrast, believed that Allied forces were not ready for such an assault. They recommended opening another front in the North African war from the west. Landings in Morocco and Algeria could, the British argued, squeeze the Axis forces in North Africa into Tunisia, where they could be destroyed or captured. After listening to lengthy discussions, President Roosevelt sided with the British. He accepted that the Allies did not have the logistics or the experience to take on the Germans in northern Europe. The new African front was given the go-ahead, and Operation Torch was developed as a combined U.S.–British campaign.

Throughout 1942 an intense argument raged between British and U.S. commanders and leaders.

The operation began on November 8, 1942 under U.S. control, with General Eisenhower as overall commander. Three landing zones were set up. The Western Task Force of 24,500 U.S. troops under Major General George S. Patton was to sail from Virginia in the United States and land around Casablanca on the coast of Morocco. The Central Task Force of 18,500 U.S. troops would sail from Britain and capture Oran on the western Algerian coast. Central Force was commanded by Major General Lloyd H.

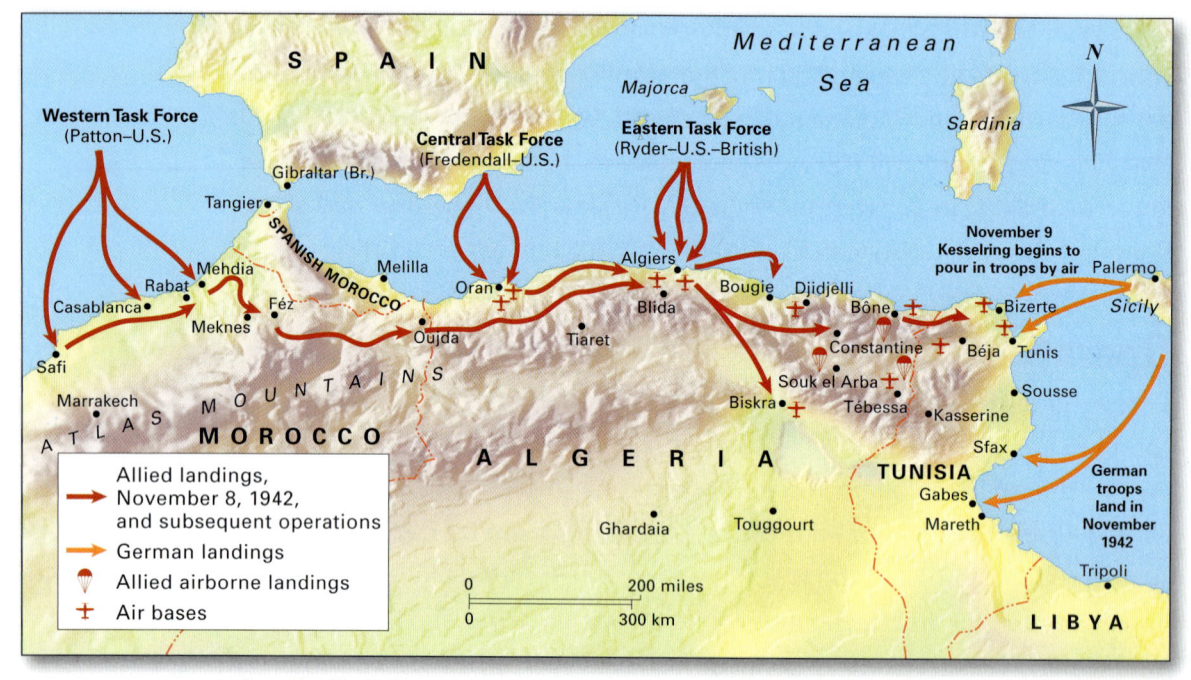

Operation Torch, November 1942, was designed to push Axis forces out of Africa.

Fredendall of the U.S. Army. The British Eastern Task Force, commanded by Major General Charles Ryder, had a mixed American and British force of 18,000 troops and was to capture Algeria's capital, Algiers.

Vichy French officials had promised that the large French garrisons in North Africa would not resist the Allied landings. The preparations for the landings were conducted in such secrecy, however, that the invasions surprised the French. Opposition emerged from French units uncertain of whom to support. The Western Task Force engaged in a naval battle with the French off the coast of Casablanca, resulting in four French warships being sunk.

At Oran, an attempt to capture the harbor using two small British ships loaded with 400 U.S. troops fell apart. French coastal guns battered the ships, killing half the sailors and soldiers; and the rest were taken prisoner. The main Oran landing went more smoothly, but troops ran into tough French resistance. The Eastern Task Force at Algiers had the most trouble-free landing of all. General Mast, the French commander in the area, cooperated with the Allies. Despite this advantage, two British destroyers met a fate similar to that of the ships in Oran harbor.

The problem of French opposition was solved on November 12 when Admiral Jean-François Darlan, foreign minister and vice premier in the Vichy government, and General Alphonse Juin, commander of French troops in Morocco, sided with the Allies. From that point on French resistance in North Africa came to an end. The Allied forces pushed hard along the northern coastline toward German defenses in Tunisia to the point at which Field Marshal Erwin Rommel's Afrika Korps was retreating.

M4 SHERMAN TANK

TECH

The introduction of the U.S. M4 Sherman tank into North Africa in 1942 gave the Allies a machine that could take on the German panzers. It was developed from the hull and suspension of the earlier M3 Medium Tank, but featured a new turret and upper hull.

Production began in late 1941, and by the end of the war U.S. plants had turned out more than 40,000 Shermans. The quantity in itself was huge, but each tank was a capable fighting machine in its own right. A standard M4 was armed with a 2.95-in. (75-mm) main gun, two 0.3-in. (7.62-mm) machine guns (one alongside the main gun, the other toward the bow), and often a 0.5-in. (12.7-mm) machine gun on the turret. The armor was up to 3 inches (76 mm) deep, though this protection still lagged behind many German tanks. The Sherman tank was easily destroyed by a shell hit.

The M4 went through extensive development. As well as battle tanks, Shermans were reconfigured into vehicles such as rocket launchers, flamethrowers, bridge-laying vehicles, and minefield clearers.

NORTH AFRICA, 1942 TO 1943   107

GENERAL GEORGE S. PATTON

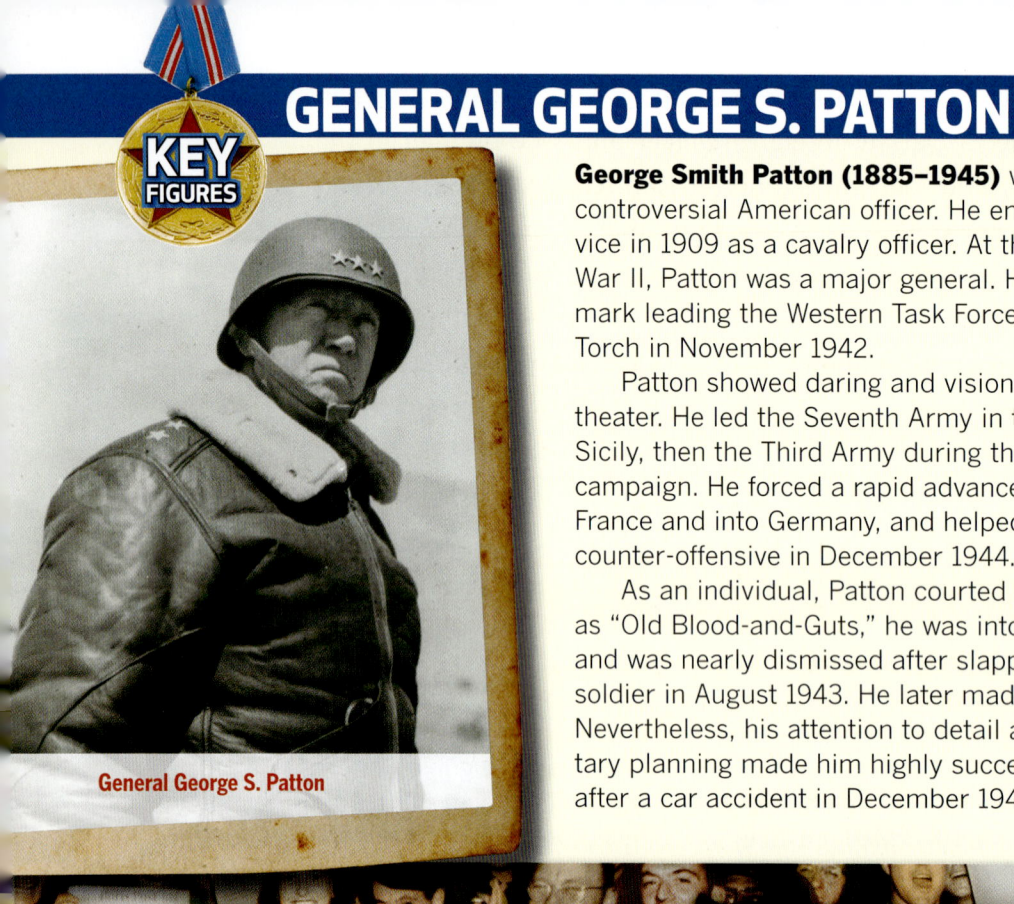

KEY FIGURES

George Smith Patton (1885–1945) was a brilliant but controversial American officer. He entered military service in 1909 as a cavalry officer. At the start of World War II, Patton was a major general. He first made his mark leading the Western Task Force during Operation Torch in November 1942.

Patton showed daring and vision in the European theater. He led the Seventh Army in the invasion of Sicily, then the Third Army during the Normandy campaign. He forced a rapid advance through occupied France and into Germany, and helped stop the German counter-offensive in December 1944.

As an individual, Patton courted controversy. Known as "Old Blood-and-Guts," he was intolerant of weakness and was nearly dismissed after slapping an American soldier in August 1943. He later made a public apology. Nevertheless, his attention to detail and rigorous military planning made him highly successful. Patton died after a car accident in December 1945.

General George S. Patton

The Battle for Tunisia

Between November 2, 1942, and January 23, 1943, Rommel's troops retreated over 1,000 miles (1,600 km) from El Alamein to Mareth. They delayed but could not stop the British Eighth Army's pursuit. By mid-February Rommel occupied the heavily defended Mareth Line in western Tunisia.

The situation soon improved for the Axis troops in Tunisia. The German High Command, which had long neglected them, now worked to stop the Allies. By early 1943, Axis troops in Tunisia numbered 250,000. New equipment bolstered the troops. Rommel was promoted to commander of all North African forces.

During November 1942, however, fewer than 5,000 combat troops were available. Nevertheless, they continued to attack. Three hundred elite German parachute soldiers attacked, captured, and held the strategic town of Medjez-el-Bab, despite being outnumbered ten to one. Other paratroopers pushed out from Bizerta and seized Djebel Abiod on the coastal road. Similar attacks gave the Germans much stronger defensive positions.

On November 25 the Allied First Army, commanded by Lieutenant General Kenneth Anderson, began a three-pronged assault. The northern and central prongs crossed the mountainous passes of northern Tunisia, and suffered heavy casualties from ambush. The southern prong managed to clear Medjez-el-Bab and Tebourba. All this territory was later recaptured.

By January 1, 1943, the Tunisian front line ran from just east of Sedjenane in the north to the Mareth Line defenses in the south. In early February German units directed their counteroffensive attack westward against the forces of Operation Torch. Montgomery's Eighth Army in the east posed less of a threat. The troops were exhausted after a 2,000-mile (3,200-km) advance and their supply lines were stretched thin. The Allied front line in Tunisia was split into three sectors: the British in the north, the French at the center, and U.S. forces in the south. Rommel joined with General Jürgen von Arnim, supreme commander of Axis Forces in Tunisia, for a decisive strike at the southern U.S. sector through to Kasserine and Tebéssa. Rommel intended to cut up north to Bône and to surround or push back the Allied forces.

The offensive was launched at 4:00 a.m. on February 14, 1943, with about 100,000 troops and nearly 300 tanks, including twelve Tigers. Arnim's 10th Panzer Division and 21st Panzer Division inflicted heavy losses on U.S. armor. Then Rommel's Afrika Korps thrust out to take Gasfa, Fériana, and Thélepte. On February 18 Arnim's and Rommel's forces met at Kasserine, in the important Western Dorsale passage. In taking Kasserine, the Germans inflicted heavy losses for the U. S. troops and dented their morale.

Kasserine was the high point of the German offensive. Afterward, it began to fall apart. Arnim and Rommel disagreed with each other. Arnim turned eastward from Kasserine to attack through Sbeitla. Rommel struck westward for Tebéssa. The Axis forces were spread thin and entering difficult terrain. By February 19 the Allies were counterattacking in force. Losses mounted, and on February 22 Rommel gave the order for a withdrawal. Kasserine was retaken by the Allies on February 25.

The February offensive cost the Germans relatively few casualties—2,000 in contrast to the Allies' 10,000. However, German losses in vehicles, fuel, and ammunition were significant, as the Allies had cut off sea and air supplies. Rommel sensed that Montgomery would begin his assault from the east on the Mareth Line, and Montgomery expected pre-emptive strikes from Rommel. In preparation, Montgomery created defensive positions around Medenine that relied on minefields and antitank weapons. On March 6 Rommel assaulted the positions, but lost over one-third of his 150 tanks, forcing him to withdraw.

Then Montgomery attacked. The southern tip of the Mareth Line rested on a long range of mountains, the Matmata Hills. Montgomery sent the New Zealand Corps over 40 miles (64 km) south of the Mareth Line to cut through a pass called Wilder's Gap on March 18–19. Once through the gap they headed north to the Tebaga Gap in the northeastern tip of the Matmata. There they would be able to flank Italian positions well behind the main eastern defenses of the Mareth Line. Then the British 50th Division would attack the Mareth Line itself.

EYEWITNESS

MALCOLM JAMES PLEYDELL

Malcolm James Pleydell, a British army doctor attached to the Special Air Service, describes the weather conditions the troops faced in North Africa.

It was blowing a sand storm; and the white grit as it swept, whistled, and eddied round the trucks, sought out each one of us, stinging, and biting, and blinding. Earlier in the morning the breeze had played over the summits of the dunes, giving them accompanying wisps of fleecy white, so that they looked like snow-capped mountains; and the sand, falling with a soft hissing, had drawn sinuous patterns on the downward slopes. Then the breeze had become a crying wind, flinging up the grains with joyful gusts so that the world became smaller and smaller, so that the jeeps and lorries disappeared from sight; and we were living in our little circle of dirty grey.

We crawled under the tarpaulin that was slung over from one side of a lorry, leaning back against it, and sitting on the loose flaps to keep them in position. Every now and then a vicious flurry of sand whisked through a hidden gap in the canvas and set us all blinking and rubbing our eyes.

Extract taken from Malcolm James Pleydell, *Born of the Desert With the SAS in North Africa* (Greenhill Books, London, 2001).

The Eighth Army's assault on the Mareth Line began on March 20, with a bombardment and infantry assault by the 50th Division. On the night of March 21 and 22 the New Zealand Corps attacked through the Tebaga Gap. The Germans responded with the 21st Panzer Division and 164th Light Division moving east to hold the Tebaga Gap and to impose heavy losses. Montgomery sent X Corps around to the Tebaga Gap to combat the breakthrough. His strategy worked. On March 26 and 27 the New Zealand Corps and 1st Armored Division (part of X Corps) plunged behind the Mareth Line. The majority of Axis forces, however, managed to escape the Allied trap. They established a defensive line in front of the New Zealand Corps and 1st Armored Division that allowed most Axis forces to flee eastward.

Once the Mareth Line had fallen, German defeat was inevitable. Rommel was ordered back to Germany, ending his North Africa campaign. By April 1943 Axis defenses were confined to a stretch of territory less than 100 miles (160 km) across in the northeastern corner of Tunisia. With pressure from all fronts, including the air and the sea, their position was hopeless. German troops were running out of food and ammunition.

In late April and early May the Eighth Army, the 18th Army Group, and First Army broke through the German lines. Bizerta and Tunis fell on May 7. Between May 8 and 12 the final Allied push cleared all enemy forces from the Cape Bon Peninsula, the northern tip of Tunisia. On May 13 the last remaining German and Italian troops in North Africa surrendered.

On May 13 the last remaining German and Italian troops in North Africa surrendered.

The North African campaign across Morocco, Algeria, and Tunisia had been a nightmare for the Allies, with 76,000 casualties and thousands of vehicles lost. Yet the Allies captured between 180,000 and 240,000 prisoners. The battles in the desert contributed greatly to the overall Allied victory in World War II. Hitler and Mussolini had sacrificed thousands of men and equipment in a lost campaign. The German troops could have better been used to protect Europe's southern flank against what was to come—the invasion of Italy.

▶ **After Pearl Harbor, Frankin Roosevelt and Winston Churchill met frequently to discuss how to help each other win the war.**

8 The Allied Plans for Victory

KEY PEOPLE	KEY PLACES	
🇬🇧 Winston Churchill	🇨🇦 Canada	🇨🇳 Moscow, Russia
🇺🇸 Franklin Delano Roosevelt	🇺🇸 Washington, D.C.	🇮🇷 Tehran, Iran
🇺🇸 General George C. Marshall	🇲🇦 Casablanca, Morocco	
🇨🇳 Joseph Stalin		

On December 11, 1941, four days after the Japanese air raid on Pearl Harbor, the dictatorships in Nazi Germany and Italy declared war on the United States. They were acting in accordance with the terms of a military alliance, the Tripartite Pact, signed with Japan in Berlin on September 27, 1940. These three nations made up the Axis powers.

The United States faced the prospect of fighting a war on both sides of the world. But the U.S. would not fight alone. Leaders in both Britain and Russia realized that with an American ally, the course of the war would turn in their favor.

Winston Churchill, Britain's prime minister, wanted to meet with U.S. president Franklin D. Roosevelt soon after Pearl Harbor. He worried that America would focus on fighting Japan and ignore the war in Europe. Churchill sent a telegram to Roosevelt on December 9 proposing to meet. The purpose, Churchill wrote, would be to study "the whole war plan." A joint approach of Britain and the United States "can best be settled on the highest executive level," meaning a personal meeting between the president and prime minister.

THE ALLIED PLANS FOR VICTORY   113

The ABC-1 Talks

Churchill had invited himself to the United States, but he knew that he would receive a warm welcome. For nearly two years the leaders had been working toward an alliance. Despite Roosevelt's public promises that the United States would not become involved in an European war, he had been sending military officers to Britain since July 1940 to develop a joint war plan against Germany. The talks between the two countries reached a peak on January 29, 1941. Known as the ABC-1 talks, the meetings proposed a joint plan of action for American and British armed forces, if and when the United States entered the war.

For nearly two years the leaders had been working toward an alliance.

The most important decision made at the ABC-1 talks was that if the United States were to go to war with both Japan and Germany, the fight against Germany—believed to be the stronger enemy and threat—would come first. The two military staffs reached this agreement a full nine months before Pearl Harbor.

The British were encouraged by the success of the ABC-1 talks. In the late summer of 1941 they tried to persuade the Americans to take a greater role in the war. Churchill and Roosevelt met to discuss this at Placentia Bay in Newfoundland, Canada, between August 10 and 15.

The British were encouraged by the success of the ABC-1 talks.

The results of the talks disappointed the British. Though Roosevelt promised to supply more military equipment and offered the help of the U.S. Navy to escort convoys across the Atlantic, he would not commit his country to war. It was a step that neither he nor U.S. military officers would consider. As Sir Alan Brooke, the British chief of staff, noted in his diary: "Not a single American officer has shown the slightest keenness to be in the war on our side. They are a charming lot of individuals but they appear to be living in a different world from ourselves." That attitude would change dramatically with the Japanese attack on the U.S. fleet at Pearl Harbor.

Arcadia

Churchill arrived in Washington, D.C., on December 22, 1941. His meeting with Roosevelt began the following day. Code-named Arcadia, the summit would be the first of seven between the two leaders. The purpose of Arcadia was to decide British and American policy for the war.

The British wanted to stay with the "Germany first" plan agreed to at ABC-1. U.S. Army chief of staff General George C. Marshall was equally eager to attack Germany. But Admiral Ernest J. King, commander in chief of the U.S. fleet, wanted to focus on Japan. The argument was settled by Roosevelt. He decided that the war against Germany was the priority.

The next question was where and how the United States would enter the war in Europe. It was agreed that the U.S. would move troops, arms, and equipment to Britain for a future attack across the English Channel. In addition, the two countries would invade North Africa from the Atlantic coast.

Many American officers objected to this plan. They wondered why, if American soldiers were supposed to be attacking Germany in Europe, they were being asked to help the British in North Africa. Some thought that the U. S. would be fighting Britain's war and not its own.

Roosevelt believed that in this first year of war the United States needed to send its troops against the enemy in Europe.

Roosevelt believed that in this first year of war the United States needed to send its troops against the enemy in Europe. However, since an attack across the French coast from England would take time to organize, he agreed with Churchill to begin an attack on the Germans and Italians in North Africa.

Now that Britain and the United States would be fighting together, they used the Arcadia talks to discuss increased cooperation between their military forces. First, the command of all Allied forces in one area of the world, such as Europe, would be given to a single officer, the supreme Allied commander. Second, staff officers from both nations would work closely together in a Combined Chiefs of Staff. This would ensure that Allied plans were followed and new ones formulated as the war went on. The Arcadia Conference ended on January 13, 1942.

THE ALLIED PLANS FOR VICTORY

GENERAL GEORGE C. MARSHALL

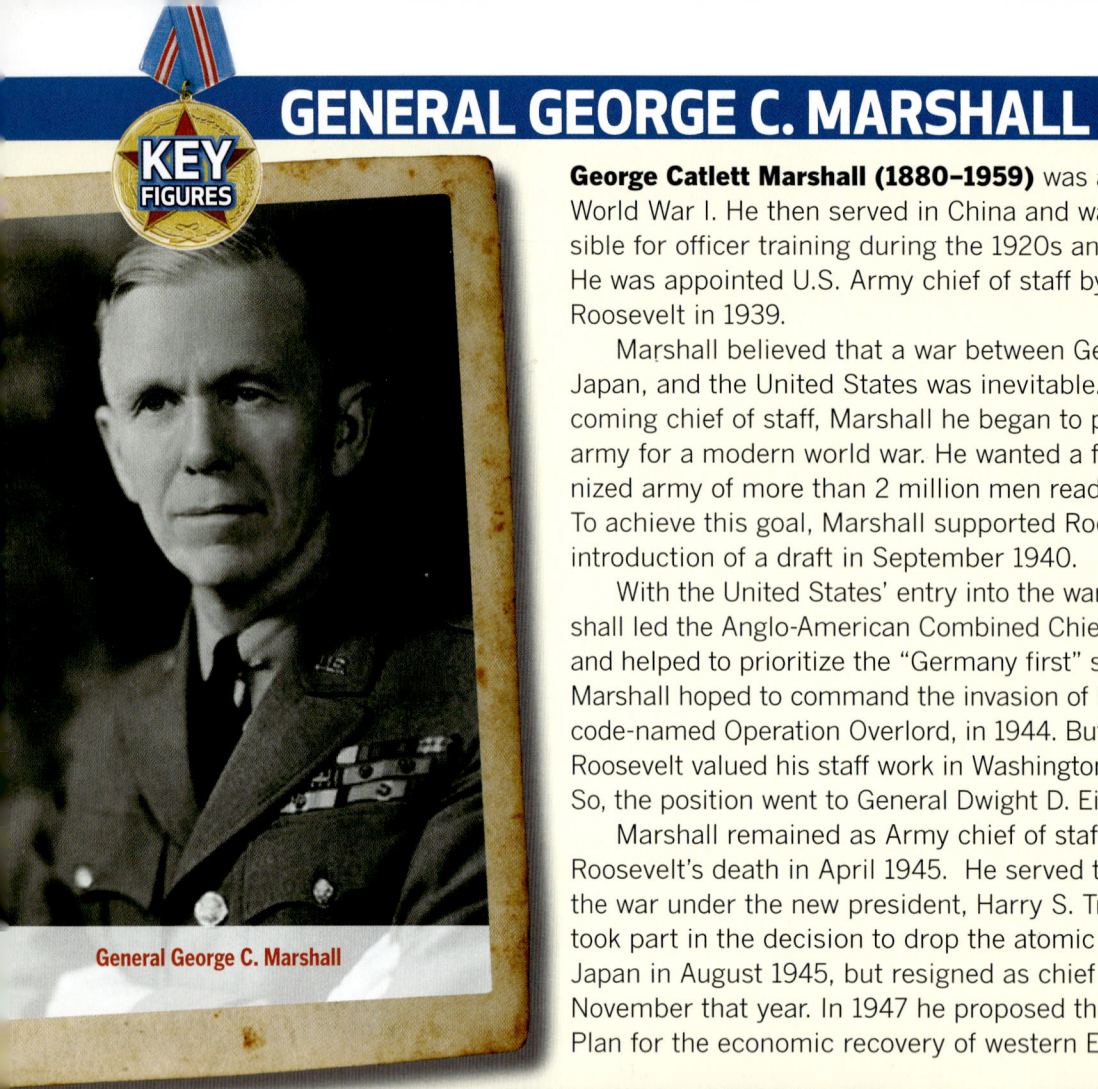

KEY FIGURES

George Catlett Marshall (1880–1959) was a veteran of World War I. He then served in China and was responsible for officer training during the 1920s and 1930s. He was appointed U.S. Army chief of staff by President Roosevelt in 1939.

Marshall believed that a war between Germany, Japan, and the United States was inevitable. On becoming chief of staff, Marshall he began to prepare the army for a modern world war. He wanted a fully mechanized army of more than 2 million men ready by 1942. To achieve this goal, Marshall supported Roosevelt's introduction of a draft in September 1940.

With the United States' entry into the war, Marshall led the Anglo-American Combined Chiefs of Staff and helped to prioritize the "Germany first" strategy. Marshall hoped to command the invasion of Europe, code-named Operation Overlord, in 1944. But President Roosevelt valued his staff work in Washington too highly. So, the position went to General Dwight D. Eisenhower.

Marshall remained as Army chief of staff after Roosevelt's death in April 1945. He served the rest of the war under the new president, Harry S. Truman. He took part in the decision to drop the atomic bomb on Japan in August 1945, but resigned as chief of staff in November that year. In 1947 he proposed the Marshall Plan for the economic recovery of western Europe.

General George C. Marshall

Casablanca

The Allied invasion of North Africa, with the code name of Operation Torch, was launched on November 8, 1942. American and British troops landed on the coasts of Morocco and Algeria and were soon advancing toward German and Italian forces in Tunisia. It proved a success. In order to make plans for the Allies' next move, Churchill asked for another conference with Roosevelt. This time it would take place in Casablanca, on Morocco's Atlantic coast.

Code-named Symbol, the Casablanca Conference took place between January 14 and 24, 1943. Publicly, the president and the prime minister were unified, but the Combined Chiefs of Staff argued about where next to attack. The British chiefs of staff believed that Allied efforts should remain concentrated in the Mediterranean. They thought victory in North Africa should be followed by an invasion north onto Sicily. They believed this plan would keep Allied troops in action against the enemy, bring about the surrender of Italy, and force the Germans to move part of their army from the Russian front.

U.S. Army officers disagreed with the British plan. They wanted to move Allied operations out of the Mediterranean and to center all efforts on an attack on Germany itself as the quickest way to win the war. U.S. Navy officers also disagreed. They wanted more men and equipment to fight against Japanese-held islands in the northern and central Pacific. After three days of argument both sides came to an agreement. The Americans would take part in the invasion of Sicily, while the British would accept an increase in the number of men the United States sent to fight the Japanese. The two sides also agreed to continue Operation Bolero—the buildup of U.S. forces in Britain. In order to ensure its success, defeating the U-boats in the Atlantic would have the highest priority to relieve the Atlantic shipping convoys trying to deliver supplies to northern Russia.

Joseph Stalin, the Russian leader, was furious when he learned that the Allies were not preparing for a full-scale invasion of Europe. He did, however, see that an attack on Italy made sense.

At the end of the Casablanca Conference, Roosevelt and Churchill, now confident of victory, met the press to discuss the agreements they had made. Roosevelt declared that the Allies' terms to end the war would be the unconditional surrender of the Axis powers. The president explained: "This does not mean the destruction of the population of Germany, Italy, or Japan, but it does mean the destruction of the philosophies in those countries which are based on the conquest and the subjugation of other people."

> *At the end of the Casablanca Conference, Roosevelt and Churchill, now confident of victory, met the press to discuss the agreements they had made.*

THE ALLIED PLANS FOR VICTORY

Trident

By the end of February 1943 the British chiefs of staff complained that the United States was breaking promises made at Casablanca. The numbers of promised U.S. troops had not arrived in Britain, and it seemed as though American war efforts were switching to the Pacific. Churchill became so concerned that in April he wrote to Roosevelt's senior political adviser, Harry Hopkins, about "grave difficulties" in Allied war plans for 1943. The prime minister called for another top-level conference.

The president, prime minister, and Combined Chiefs of Staff met in Washington, D.C., between May 12 and 25, 1943. Code-named Trident, the conference was filled with hard bargaining. The Americans showed that their greater role in the war had made them the senior partner in the alliance.

The British agreed to a date for the invasion of France: May 1, 1944. The attack on Sicily would go ahead during the summer of 1943. Churchill still believed an invasion of the Italian mainland would be the next logical move against the Axis.

The Combined Chiefs of Staff accepted plans for a bombing offensive to be launched from Britain against German cities. The offensive would be carried out by Britain's RAF Bomber Command and the U.S. Army Eighth Air Force. Known as Operation Point Blank, it would begin in June 1943. Churchill and Roosevelt also agreed that the United States and Britain should work together to develop the atomic bomb. Work would take place in the United States.

Quadrant

The invasion of Sicily, code-named Operation Husky, took place on July 10, 1943. By August 12 German troops were retreating from the island to the Italian mainland across the Straits of Messina. By August 14 the Italians were asking the Allies for terms of surrender. Victory in Sicily encouraged Churchill to ask for another conference with Roosevelt, in order to win backing for more operations in the Mediterranean. This meeting, the so-called Quadrant Conference, took place during August 13–23 in Quebec, Canada.

The British wanted the Americans to agree to a joint invasion of the Italian mainland and capture of the capital, Rome. Churchill and his chiefs of staff were eager to extend the Mediterranean war east into Greece, in the hope of bringing neutral Turkey into the war on the Allied side. Roosevelt's staff, including Marshall, agreed to the Italian invasion. Roosevelt went no further, though. He declined to commit U.S. troops to the Greek islands.

POLITICAL WORLD: THE SECOND FRONT DEBATE

One question dominated the conferences and talks among the Allies in 1942 and 1943. When would Britain and the United States invade occupied France and open a second front?

A popular campaign in Britain by the press had promoted the opening of a second front since Hitler's invasion of Russia in June 1941. The entry of the United States into the war in December 1941 changed the situation. By April 1942 General George C. Marshall was in London to present the British with a plan of action. It called for an attack across the English Channel toward Germany—code-named Operation Roundup—to take place in the summer of 1943.

A smaller operation, code-named Operation Sledgehammer, would take place in the fall of 1942. Operation Sledgehammer would exploit a sudden collapse of the German army to halt the defeat of the Soviet Union. Whichever plan was chosen, the Americans wanted to set a decision and a date for attack.

The British accepted that an attack into Germany across the English Channel was essential. Still, they needed to continue their defense of North Africa. They were also worried that if an invasion took place without proper planning, lives would be thrown away. During the Allied conferences of 1942 and 1943, they postponed agreeing to an invasion date.

In 1942 Operation Sledgehammer was canceled in favor of Operation Torch, the Anglo-American invasion of Morocco and Algeria. By the end of 1942, Operation Roundup moved from the summer of 1943 to the fall. Churchill told Stalin that it was the result of "the crippling lack of shipping," but that plans for the invasion were being "kept alive from week to week." Stalin was unimpressed. Why should shipping delay an attack? "Why can't you send in your men by parachute?" he asked.

By 1943 the British and American war effort was concentrated on Sicily and Italy. By the time of the Trident Conference in May, even Roosevelt had to admit that a cross-channel attack was not possible that year. Roundup, soon to be renamed Operation Overlord, would be pushed back to May 1944. Even then Churchill did not seem satisfied. At the Tehran Conference in December Churchill suggested postponing the date to July 1944. However, Roosevelt and Stalin would not hear of any more delays. Operation Overlord would take place in the summer of 1944.

U.S. Army vehicles unload from a landing craft during the invasion of Sicily, July 1943.

The Quadrant Conference provided the American delegates with an opportunity to plot the invasion of France, code-named Operation Overlord. Some of the most experienced combat units were to be transferred from the Mediterranean to Britain for training. The original estimate of troop numbers for Operation Overlord was increased by about 25 percent. A diversionary attack along the coast of southern France would be planned for the same time.

The Moscow Conference

Quadrant was the fourth meeting between Churchill and Roosevelt and their staffs since January 1942. The third Allied power, Russia, had not yet been at a meeting. Stalin had been invited to Casablanca in January 1943, but had refused. Churchill had also invited him to talks in Iceland, and Roosevelt had suggested a meeting in Alaska. Stalin had turned down both offers.

After Quadrant, and with Allied victory in Europe inching closer, Stalin proposed a meeting of the Allied foreign ministers in the Russian capital, Moscow. There they would prepare for the first full summit meeting between Roosevelt, Churchill, and Stalin, popularly known as the "Big Three."

POLITICAL WORLD: ALLIES AND ADVERSARIES

The key western Allies, the United States and Britain, were committed to the defeat of Germany, Italy, and Japan in World War II. Each had an agenda, though, that generated possibilities for friction. In the critical period of 1942 and 1943, common needs usually kept them together. Still, there were disputes.

The two nations had a basic difference in the way that they wished to fight the war in Europe. The United States believed that the defeat of Germany was the quickest way to win the war. The British disagreed: they argued for attacks on Axis possessions in Europe, such as Norway, the Dodecanese Islands in the Mediterranean, or the Balkans. The British got their way in the decision to invade Italy, even though it was a campaign that moved slowly up the mountainous peninsula.

The British argument for the invasion of Italy was phrased in terms of the difficulties of landing an army in France. Such a landing would be disastrous if it failed. However, three other factors supported British arguments. The first lay in history. In British military history there was a long tradition of the "indirect approach"—using naval power to land troops where they could do damage to an enemy without engaging in major land actions. The main exception to this had been during World War I. The huge losses on the western front had scarred the memories of all who had seen the carnage. These officers were the men running the British military during World War II.

This "indirect approach" was associated with the second factor. Britain faced a manpower crisis from mid-1943 onward. They did not have sufficient men to fill the ranks of a mass army while still trying to maintain industrial production. In 1943, for example, women were no longer recruited for the British armed forces because they were more important to supplement the industrial labor force. Mass battles in western Europe required a mass army able to absorb heavy casualties. Therefore, Britain's role in such battles would be less than that of countries with bigger manpower reserves.

These factors in turn led to the third underlying factor: Britain wished to maintain its role as a great power after the war. From this perspective, establishing British control of the Middle East and the eastern Mediterranean was more important than a U.S.-dominated victory in western Europe. This final factor was clear to U.S. war leaders, and they would have none of it. They believed the key war aim was to defeat the Nazi State, not to help Britain retain its overseas empire.

The Moscow Conference of foreign ministers took place between October 20 and 31, 1943. It involved the American secretary of state, Cordell Hull, the British foreign secretary, Sir Anthony Eden, and the Soviet foreign minister, Vyacheslav Molotov. They discussed the proposed dates for Operation Overlord and the proposed Big Three meeting. The meeting was scheduled to take place in Tehran, Iran, in late November. Tehran had been suggested by the Russians because, occupied by Russian troops, it was safe for Stalin to visit.

Sextant

Roosevelt and Churchill and their staffs would have one more round of talks before they met Stalin in Tehran. During their journey toward Iran, the two Allied leaders held a meeting in Cairo. Code-named Sextant, the conference took place between November 23 and 26, 1943.

Sextant proved to be another difficult meeting for the British. Churchill insisted that the war could be won more quickly with attacks in the eastern Mediterranean. The Americans, especially General Marshall, lost their patience. Roosevelt still wanted instead to concentrate on the war against Japan in the Pacific. The president had invited the leader of the Chinese nationalists, Jiang Jieshi to the conference, and Churchill was forced to spend time talking about a possible offensive in northern Burma. The conference broke up after three days of discussion. The leaders could make no important decisions until the Tehran meeting with Stalin a few days later.

The "Big Three"

The Tehran conference, code-named Eureka, began on November 28, 1943, and ended December 1. At it, the Allies decided the war plans for 1944. Stalin's only interest during Eureka was the timing of Operation Overlord, and the British and American efforts to make it happen. Stalin accepted May 1, 1944, as the proposed invasion date. He also supported plans for a diversionary attack on the coast of southern France. Stalin also asked that Roosevelt name the commanding officer of Operation Overlord.

The "Big Three," Stalin, Roosevelt, and Churchill (*left to right*), debated Allied war strategy in several meetings during 1943.

Stalin made two important promises to the Americans and British. Russia would launch a major offensive on the eastern front at the same time as Operation Overlord. Russia also would join in the war against Japan as soon as Germany was defeated.

After leaving Tehran, Roosevelt, Churchill and the Combined Chiefs of Staff met again in Cairo between December 4 and 6 to discuss the meeting with Stalin. It was decided that Operation Overlord and the diversionary attack on southern France, now code-named Operation Anvil, would take priority. The British offered no more talks about the Mediterranean theater. Roosevelt also announced that the commander of Operation Overlord would be U.S. Army General Dwight D. Eisenhower.

The president left Cairo for the United States on December 7. The Allies' war plans for 1944 were set. Churchill and Roosevelt would not meet again until after Operation Overlord in 1944.

Timeline

1942
- Roosevelt and Churchill plan military action against Axis-occupied Europe.
- Japan attacks the Philippines and the Dutch East Indies.
- Japan invades Burma.
- Germans begin Operation Drum Roll.
- The Wannsee Conference adopts "The Final Solution."
- Rommel launches offensive in Libya.
- U. S. carriers attack the Marshall and Gilbert Islands.
- Singapore is lost to the Japanese.
- U.S. and Filipino forces surrender to Japanese on Bataan.
- Japanese forces capture Lashio and cut the Burma Road.
- Japan attacks Allies in the Coral Sea; Japan's code broken.
- U.S. and Filipino forces surrender Corregidor.
- Carrier aircraft battle in Coral Sea.
- Germany's Eleventh Army clashes with Soviets in Crimea.
- Rommel attacks the Gazala Line in Libya.
- Britain launches "1,000-bomber" raid against Cologne, Germany.
- Japanese attack U.S. base in the Battle of Midway.
- Rommel captures Tobruk; the Allies retreat to Egypt.
- Germans seize Voronezsh.
- Germans siege Sevastopol.
- German Army Group A captures Rostov; advance into the Caucasus.
- U. S. Marines land on Guadalcanal.
- Luftwaffe attacks Stalingrad.
- Allies win first major victory of war at El Alamein, Egypt.
- Axis forces occupy Vichy France.
- Soviets attack Germans at Stalingrad; trap the Sixth Army.
- U. S. scientists create first "chain reaction"; develop atomic bomb.

1943
- U.S. forces land on New Guinea.
- Japanese evacuate troops from Guadalcanal.
- Rommel abandons Tripoli.
- Jews erupt in Warsaw ghetto.
- British bombers make first daylight raid over Berlin.
- Germany's Sixth Army surrenders at Stalingrad.
- Soviets recapture Kursk, Krasnodar, and Rostov in Ukraine.
- Rommel routs U. S. II Corps, then withdraws.
- Soviets liberate Kharkov, Ukraine.
- Allied Chindits conduct first jungle warfare mission in Burma.
- U. S. and Australians fight Japanese in the Battle of the Bismark Sea.
- German troops rebuffed south of Mareth Line; Rommel leaves Africa.
- German forces destroy Soviet Third Tank Army and recapture Kharkov and Belgorod.
- Axis forces in Tunisia surrender.
- Dönitz suspends U-boat patrols in northern Atlantic.
- Axis troops attack Yugoslavia.
- Allied bombers launch Operation Pointblank against Germany.
- U.S. troops land on New Georgia Islands in the Solomons.
- German and Red Army troops and armor clash at Kursk.
- U.S. bombers attack oil fields in Romania.
- German and Italian forces withdraw from Sicily.
- Italy surrenders; German forces occupy northern Italy.
- U-boats begin operations again.
- Japanese complete Burma–Siam railroad, using Allied prisoners.
- Allies land on New Britain.

124 HORRIFIC INVASIONS

Bibliography

Beevor, Antony. *Stalingrad: The Fateful Siege.* New York: Penguin, 1999.

Bicheno, Hugh. *Midway.* New York: Sterling Publishing Company, 2002.

Donovan, Robert J. *P T-109, John F. Kennedy in World War II.* Columbus, Ohio: McGraw-Hill, 1961.

Dyess, William E. *Bataan Death March: A Survivor's Account.* Lincoln, Nebraska: University of Nebraska Press, 2002.

D'Este, Carlo. *Patton: A Genius for War.* New York: Perennial, 1996.

Ellis, Chris. *21st Panzer Division: Rommel's Afrika Korps Spearhead.* Hersham, UK: Ian Allan Publishing, 2002.

Ford, Roger. *The Sherman Tank.* St. Paul, Minnesota: Motorbooks International, 1999.

Frank, Richard B. *Guadalcanal: The Definitive Account of the Landmark Battle.* New York: Penguin, 1992.

Kimball, Warren F. *Forged in War: Roosevelt, Churchill, and the Second World War.* New York: Ivan R. Dee, Inc., 2003.

Latimer, Jon. *Alamein.* Cambridge, Massachusetts: Harvard University Press, 2002.

Manchester, William. *American Caesar: Douglas MacArthur 1880–1963.* New York: Laureleaf, 1996.

McGee, William. *The Solomons Campaign, 1942–1943.* Sanata Barbara, California: BMC Publications, 2001.

Moorhead, Alan, and John Keegan. *Desert War: The North African Campaign, 1940–1943.* New York: Penguin, 2001.

Morison, Samuel Eliot. *Operations in North African Waters: October 1942–June 1943.* New York: Book Sales, Inc., 2001.

———. *Aleutians, Gilberts, and Marshalls, June 1942–April 1944.* New York: Book Sales, Inc., 2001.

Morton, Louis. *United States Army in World War II: Fall of the Philippines.* Washington, D.C.: Government Printing Office, 1998.

Murray, Williamson. *Luftwaffe, 1933–45.* Dulles, Virginia: Brasseys, 1996.

Patton, George S. *War As I Knew It.* New York: Mariner Books (Houghton Mifflin), 1995.

Potter, Elmer Belmont. *Nimitz.* Annapolis, Maryland: The Unites States Naval Institute Press, 1988.

Rommel, Erwin, et al. *The Rommel Papers.* New York: Da Capo Press, 1988.

Smith, Denis Mack. *Mussolini.* New York: Sterling Publications, 2002.

Speer, Albert, et al. *Inside the Third Reich: Memoirs.* New York: Touchstone Books, 1997.

Stein, George H. *The Waffen SS: Hitler's Elite Guard at War, 1939–1945.* Ithaca, New York: Cornell University Press, 2001.

Tregaskis, Richard. *Guadalcanal Diary.* New York: The Modern Library, 2000.

Voss, Johan. *Black Edelweiss: A Memoir of Combat and Conscience by a Soldier of the Waffen-SS.* Bedford, Pennsylvania: The Aberjona Press, 2002.

Werner, Herbert A. *Iron Coffins: A Personal Account of the German U-Boat Battles of World War II.* New York: Henry Holt, 1969.

Further Information

BOOKS

Elish, Dan. *Franklin Delano Roosevelt* (Presidents and Their Times). New York: Marshall Cavendish, 2009.

Horner, David. *World War II: The Pacific* (Essential Histories). New York: Rosen, 2010.

Jensen, Richard, and Tim McNeese, eds. *World War II 1939-1945* (Discovering U.S. History). New York: Chelsea House, 2010.

Williams, Barbara. *World War II: Pacific* (Chronicle of America's Wars). Minneapolis: Lerner Publications, 2004.

WEBSITES

www.wwiimemorial.com
The U.S. National World War II Memorial.

www.hitler.org
The Hitler Historical Museum is a nonpolitical, educational resource for the study of Hitler and Nazism.

http://gi.grolier.com/wwii/wwii_ mainpage.html
The story of World War II, with biographies, articles, photographs, and films.

www.ibiblio.org/pha
Original documents on all aspects of the war.

DVDS

Great Fighting Machines of World War II. Arts Magic, 2007.

The War: A Film by Ken Burns and Lynn Novick. PBS Home Video, 2007.

World War II 360°. A & E Television Networks, 2009.

Index

NOTE: Page numbers in *italics* refer to pictures or their captions. WWI refers to World War I. Page numbers in **bold** refer to photographs or illustrations.

A

ABC-1 talks, 114
Akagi (carrier), **29**
El Alamein, Egypt, 100, 101–105
Alam Halfa, Battle of, 103
Aleutian Islands, **18, 23,** 25–26, 64–65
Alexander, Harold, 40, 103
Allies, 8, 113–123
American Volunteer Group, 44
amphibious warfare, 60–63, 65
Anderson, Kenneth, 109
Arakan, Philippines, 48–49
Arcadia Conference, 115
Arnim, Jürgen von, 109
Asia. *See* East Asia; *specific countries*
atomic weapons, 16, 91, 116, 118
Attu, Aleutians Islands, 64–65
Auchinleck, Claude, 97, 98–103
Australia, 18
  and Kennedy, 59
  land forces, 32, 52–54, 102
  POWs in Burma, 86
  warships, 12, 34, 46, 53

B

Bataan Peninsula, **14,** 15–19
Belgium, 83, 90
Bismarck Sea, Battle of the, 53
Bloody Ridge, Battle of, 32–33
Bock, Feodor von, 69
Borneo, 85
Bougainville, Solomons, 58–60
Brooke, Sir Alan, 114
Burma (Myanmar), 39, 40–42, 45, 47–49, 86, 95
Burma Road, **38,** 49

C

Casablanca, Morocco, 51, 116–117
Caucasus, 69, 70, 72
Ceylon (Sri Lanka), 45
Chennault, Claire, 44, 49
China, 39, 40, 42–43, 45, 49, 86
Chindits, the, 47
Chuikov, Vasily, 71–73
Churchill, Winston, **51,** 103, **112,** 113–**123**
Coral Sea, Battle of the, 22, 24–25
Corregidor, **14,** 15, 17–18
Crimean Peninsula, 69–70
Croatia, 89
Cyrenaica, Libya, 98–100
Czechoslovakia, 85

D

Denmark, 83
Doorman, Karel, 12
Dutch East Indies, 10, 12, 85
Dutch Nazi Party, 89

E

East Asia, 81, 85–86, 89, 94–95. *See also specific countries*
Eisenhower, Dwight D., 105
Eureka Conference, 122–123
Europe, 67, **80,** 82–85, 88–92, 94. *See also specific countries*

F

Finschhafen, 31, **53, 55,** 58–59
Flying Tigers, 44, 49
France, 83, 85, 87, 90, 91
Fredendall, Lloyd H., 105–106
Friedman, William, 64
Fuchida, Mitsuo, 28

G

Gazala Line, 98–100
Germany
  Allies' bombing campaign, 118
  Gestapo, 84
  Hitler, 68–70, 72, 74–75, 79–80
  and resistance, **80,** 85, 90–92, 94
  territories occupied by, 81, 82–83, 84, 92
  Waffen SS, 75, 77, 78, 90, 92
  See also Soviet Union, German invasion of
Ghormley, Robert, 31
Gilberts, the, 60–63
Goebbels, Joseph, 67
Göring, Hermann, 74
Great Britain
  and Burma, 39, 42, 45
  military strategy, 6, 48–49, 119, 121
  and resistance, 90, 93, 95
  See also North Africa
Greece, 89
Griswold, Oscar, 56
Guadalcanal, **20,** 31–35, 37, 52, **55**

Guam, 15
Guderian, Heinz, 77

H

Halsey, William, 35, 52, 55–58
Herring, Edmund, 32
Hitler, Adolf, 68–70, 72, 74–75, 79–80
Homma, Masaharu, 15–19
Hong Kong, 6, 85
Hungarian forces, 69, 70
Hutton, Thomas, 40

I

Iida, Shijiro, 40–41, 48–49
India, 42, 45
Indian Ocean, 45–46
Indochina, **4,** 5, 86
Italian forces, 69, 70, 74, **76, 102**
Italy, **82,** 94

J

Japan, **4**
  and Burma, 39, 40–41, 42, 45
  and Dutch East Indies, 10, 12
  military strategy, 5–6, 11, 14–15, 21–36, 37, 45–46, 51–52, 113
  and Philippines, 15–19
  and resistance, 94–95
  territories occupied by, 6, 8, 9, 81, 85–86
Java Sea, Battle of the, 12
Jiang Jieshi, 40, 43, 122

K

Kennedy, John F., 59
Kenney, George, 53
Kharkov, Russia, 75–76
King, Ernest J., 30–31, 115
Kinkaid, Thomas, 35, 65
Kiska, Aleutians Islands, 64–65
Kittyhawk aircraft, 44
Kluge, Gunther von, 77, 78
Komandorski Islands, Battle of the, 65
Kondo, Nobutake, 26, 30, 35, 45
Kosaka, Jinichi, 52
Kurst, Russia, 77–78

L

Lae, New Guinea, 53–54

INDEX 127

Lashio, Burma, 41, 42
Leningrad, Russia, 68
Lexington (carrier), **24,** 25
Libya, 98–100
List, Wilhelm, 72
Luftwaffe, 68, 69
Luzon, Philippines, 15–17

M
MacArthur, Douglas, 15–17, 30–32, 52–54
Macassar Strait, 10, 12
Magic code breakers, 64, **101**
Makin, the Gilberts, 60, 62
Malaya (Malaysia), 8, 85–86, 95
Malta, 97, 98
Manchuria, 86
Mandalay, Burma, **42**
Manstein, Erich von, 69–70, 74, 75, 78, 79
Maquis resistance fighters, 91
Mareth Line, Tunisia, **106,** 108–111, 109, 110
Marshall, George Catlett, 105, 116
Midway, 15, **23,** 25–30
Montgomery, Bernard, 103–104, 109
Morocco, 51, 105–106, 116–117
Moscow Conference, 120–122

N
Nagano, Osami, 21, 22
Nagumo, Chuichi, 26, 27, 29
Netherlands, **80,** 89
New Britain, 54. *See also* Rabaul
New Georgia, 55–56, 58
New Guinea, 31–32, 52–54, **55,** 58–59, 85
New Zealand forces, 104, 110–111
Nimitz, Chester, 26, 36, 51, 60
North Africa, **96, 106**
    El Alamein, 100–105
    Libya, 98–100
    Tunisia, 107, 108–111
    U.S.–British campaign, 105–107, 115, 119
Norway, 87, 88, 91

O
Office of Strategic Services, 93
Oradour-sur-Glane, France, 85
Ozawa, Jisaburo, 45–46

P
paratroopers, 108–109
Parker, George, 15–16
Patch, Alexander, 33
Patton, George S., 105, 108
Paulus, Friedrich von, 70, 71–72, 74–75
Pearl Harbor attack, 5–6, 11, 113

Percival, Arthur, 8, 9
Pétain, Philippe, 88
Philippines, 15–19, 94–95
Pleydell, Malcolm James, 110
Poland, 83, 84, 87, 88, 92
Polish Home Army, 92
PT 109, 59

Q
Quadrant Conference, 118–120
Quisling, Vidkun, 87, 88

R
Rabaul, New Britain, **18, 55**
    and Battle of the Coral Sea, 22
    Japan's base on, 51–53, 54, 57
    U.S. strategy for recapture, 31, 58–59
Rangoon (Yangon), Burma, 40
resistance movements, **80,** 85, 90–92, 94–95
Ritchie, Neil, 100
Romanian forces, 69, 70, 74
Rommel, Erwin, 97, 98–105, 108–111, **101**
Roosevelt, Franklin D., **51, 112,** 113–**123**
Rotem, Simha, 89
Russell Islands, 55
Russia. *See* Soviet Union
Ryder, Charles, 106

S
Santa Cruz Islands, Battle of, 34–35
Savo Island, Battle of, 34
Sevastopol, Crimean Peninsula, 69–70
Sextant Conference, 122
Siam (Thailand), 39, **41**
Sicily, **106,** 108, 117–119, **120**
Singapore, 9, 85, 86, 95
Slim, William, 40
Solomon Islands, 30–32, 54–56, 58–60
Somerville, James, 45–46
Soviet Union, **66**
    overview, 67
    Stalin and, 92, 105, 117, 119–123
    summer offensives, 78–79
    Ukraine, 88
Soviet Union, German invasion of
    Crimean Peninsula, 69–70
    Kharkov, 75–76
    Kurst, 77–78
    Leningrad, 68
    occupied territories, 84, 92
    Stalingrad, 70–75
Special Operations Executive, 93
Spruance, Raymond, 60–63
Stalin, Joseph, 92, 105, 117, 119–**123**

Stalingrad, Russia, 70–75
Stilwell, Joseph, 40, 43, 46, 49
submarine warfare, **23,** 26, 30, 34, 62

T
Takagi, Takeo, 22, 24
tank warfare, **96,** 99, 102, 104, 107. *See also* North Africa
Taranto, Battle of, 23
Tarawa, the Gilberts, 60–61, 63
Tehran Conference, 122–123
Thailand, 89, 95
Thailand-Burma railroad, 86
Timor, 85
Timoshenko, Semyon, 70
Tobruk, Libya, 99–101
Trident Conference, 118
Tunisia, **106,** 107, 108–111

U
Ukraine, 88
United States
    military strategy, 31, 58–59, 105–107, 114–115, 119
    Pacific bases, 14–19
    and resistance, 90, 93, 95
    tanks built in, 99, 102, 104, 107
    warships, 22, 24–25, 26, 28–29, **31,** 34–35
U.S. China Air Task Force, 44
U.S. Marines, **20,** 32–33, 54, 58, 63

V
Vandegrift, Alexander, 32–33, 58
Vella Lavella, Solomon Islands, 58
Vichy France, 86, 88, 106–107

W
Waffen SS, 75, 77, 78, 90, 92
Wainwright, Jonathan, 15
Wake Island, 14
Waldron, John, 28
Wavell, Archibald, 8, 46, 48
Weichs, Maximilian von, 71
Wingate, Orde, 47

Y
Yamamoto, Isoroku
    and Japanese military strategy, 21, 22, 25–26, 35
    overview, 13, 52
    on Pearl Harbor, 5, 11
Yamashita, Tomoyuki, 8, 9
Yugoslavia, 92, 94
Yunnan, China, 44, 45, 49

Z
Zhukov, Georgi, 68, 72